Uneasy Rider: Confessions of a Reluctant Traveller

Allie Sommerville

Published in 2009 by New Generation Publishing

Copyright © Allie Sommerville

First Edition

The author asserts the moral right under the Copyright, Designs and Patents Act 1988 to be identified as the author of this work.

All Rights reserved. No part of this publication may be reproduced, stored in a retrieval system or transmitted, in any form or by any means without the prior consent of the author, nor be otherwise circulated in any form of binding or cover other than that which it is published and without a similar condition being imposed on the subsequent purchaser.

Published by New Generation Publishing

Thanks!

I'd like to thank everyone on Harper Collins writer's forum, Authonomy, for the support, advice and encouragement freely given by its members.

Impossible to mention everyone, but especially (and in no particular order):

Jeff Blackmer
John Booth
Nicky Forshaw (Nix)
Michael Scott (Absolution)
Sue Edwards (Little Devil)
Craig Edwards
Denise Hunt (DeniseJane)
JD Revene
Lillian Kendrick (Verse Artist)
Traci York (InternetG33k)
T. Staz
Charles Utley (Cutley)
Raven Dane (Morven)
Ed Quinn
Phillip Gilliver
Doctor Anthony Saunders

Big thanks go to Cameron Chapman for doing the formatting

And not forgetting Bradley Wind who has given so much of his time and expertise to creating fantastic covers for so many books on Authonomy – mine included!

Contents

Warning! This book is a collection of themed chapters chronicling several trips and therefore can be read in any order. It is not a guidebook.

1	**"No Woman, No Cry"** ... If you're of a nervous disposition, don't travel in May	1
2	**The Parable of a Parador** ... Why it's not always a good idea to get a wish fulfilled	10
3	**Inauguration of the Innocent** ... "Beam me up ..."	26
4	**On How To Find...a Campsite** ... Not as easy as you might think	36
5	**Space-Tales from Under the Awning** ... Time And Relative Dimensions (on site)	42
6	***Et In Arcadia Ego*** ... Staying on the dark side	48
7	***Et in Aranjuez Ego*** ... A paler shade of dark	55
8	**"...we've got a problem..." Part the first** ... Small Problems	59
9	**"...we've got a problem..." Part the second** ... Bigger emergencies	68
10	**An Arpeggio on the Campeggio** ... *La Dolce Vita* on a Florentine campsite	77

11	**Noises Off** … Always something there to annoy us	*109*
12	**More Noises & Other Nuisances** … More noises and other nuisances	*114*
13	**A Hitch-Hiker Guides … to Montserrat** … For once, a good turn is unpunished	*120*
14	**When in Rome** … Trials and tribulations in the Eternal City	*130*
15	**Shouting in the Sistine** … The Vatican's a funny old place	*141*
16	**Money, Money, Money** … Down but not out in Casino… and elsewhere	*147*
17	*Cave Canem* … Dogs, mushrooms, ruins in Pompeii	*157*
18	**Venice - Vaporetti & Victimisation** … A Grand Time on the Grand Canal and a Put Down in Punta Sabbioni	*163*
19	**All Our Pitches are Flat** … as is Holland	*172*
20	**Willcommen, Bienvenido, Welcome** … or not as the case may be	*176*
21	**Apes, Rocks and Pizza** … The ins and outs of Gibraltar	*182*
22	**Fuentes!** … and a diary of our final days in Spain	*187*
23	**Top Ten Tips** … for what they're worth	*196*

"No Woman, No Cry"
High Anxieties

If we were unsure of our van's height before, going through the underpass at *Puzol* left us with some clue as to what it was. The look on the face of the woman driving towards us from the other end said it all. *Don't attempt to get under anything lower than 3 metres high again.* Considering the palaver of the past week or so, it was hardly surprising we'd taken a chance.

Religiously following directions to anything marked *Camping* became our mission in life during our time in Spain. During this, our first trip, the prospect of 'wild camping' loomed over me like the huge spaceship in the film *Independence Day*. The word *wild* did not appeal at all to my delicate nature. We'd become accustomed to the plethora of campsites vying for our business in France, some of them even open, but the arrangements in Spain at the end of May were less than adequate. Since crossing the border, a visible signpost to such places was a much-prized rarity and something to be remarked upon. Not unusual though was that having spotted such a sign, we could easily travel miles before realising that hoping to find another was futile. About as futile as the UK hoping to win the *Eurovision Song Contest* ever again even with Lord Lloyd Webber on board. Anyway, by the time we'd realised this, we would probably have reached the outskirts of the next town. The blood-red Spanish sun would be clawing its way down below the distant horizon, remarkably resembling the *Catalan* flag. Disappearing with it would be my slight bit of confidence that we too would find a place to rest. Let alone what I would deem a safe one.

Our unplanned circumnavigation of the area near the attractively scaffolded and tower-craned town of *Puçol* near *Valencia* on the *Costa Blanca*, eventually resulted in the sighting of a postage stamp weakly proclaiming 'Camping' in faded brown letters. It grudgingly pointed straight ahead. All well and good you might think, but our relief was short lived. What lay ahead was not a good prospect: a low underpass under the railway. This railway divided the town, and the underpass was its main through route. We were in no mood to find another way round to get to the campsite, and getting lost again was not an option I wanted to explore.

Harry pulled the van to one side in front of the tunnel entrance. Since the previous owner had added various vents to the roof in such a random manner, it was difficult to tell exactly where and what the highest point was.

"Well what do you think?" I asked my all-knowing Other Half.

"It should be OK..." Harry replied, but I didn't like the slight tone of doubt in his voice. "...the height restriction SAYS 2.8 metres. Our handbook says the van is 2.7."

"So what is it?"

"Your guess is as good as..."

I stopped him there.

"I don't want to guess, I want to *know*," I said meaningfully.

With that, he put the engine into gear and I held my breath, as if that would have helped. We plunged into the depths and listened for scraping sounds. That lady in the *SEAT* driving towards us would certainly have a tale to tell her family when she arrived home. *Those stupid English tourists in their camper vans*! This unfortunately was only the prologue to another disconcerting episode at *Puçol*.

Whilst risking the underpass did not entirely solve our problem in getting to our overnight stopping place, eventually we came across a site that we assumed was the one indicated pre-tunnel. It may well have been, but seeing as it resembled a Wild West ghost town, almost down to that bushy stuff blowing around, we realised that it wasn't open for business. Our appearance on site however attracted the last human alive in Dodge City (the undertaker?) and he directed us along the road to a campsite that was *definitely* open. Well of course the only obvious way to get to this site was along a one-way street, the wrong way, but by this time we were past caring. Again the place looked like Jessie James and his gang had recently paid a visit, but undeterred we cruised around the large, walled site to find an empty pitch to stay on for the night. It may seem a paradox in that an empty site contained few vacant pitches, so for anyone who has never visited any Spanish campsites within a reasonable driving distance from a large town or city such as Barcelona, please let me explain.

Forget idyllic scenes of open fields and rolling countryside with hardy outdoor-types enjoying the fresh air; think more Brazilian shanty-town. These places are for the most part filled with makeshift 'semi-permanent' dwellings. Caravans that couldn't have seen a road since before Franco's time are cobbled together with tents, awnings and sheds, the antiquity of which made me wonder if they'd served some fearsome purpose during the Spanish Inquisition. Each establishment has scarcely a few inches between it and its neighbour, a sight which would be enough to give a collective heart attack to members of any British camping or caravanning club with their optimistic '*20-foot-space-between-each-unit*' rule. We might think these cramped Spanish arrangements highly undesirable, but it appears that the *Catalans* in particular love such communal living. All the family, from the most gnarled ancient to the newest infant, squeeze happily into these modest and haphazard structures, and a jolly time is had by all. At dusk during low-season though, these shuttered and empty dwellings reminded me of those scenes in SciFi movies where some alien has spirited everyone away. But then I am always getting carried away too.

Back at the deserted maze that was the campsite at *Puçol*, we were approached by a man who seemed to be something to do with the place, in that he was Spanish and in his overalls looked like some sort of workman. At last here was someone we could speak to about staying on the site. Although I say 'speak', this is not quite the description of our communication, my Spanish skills at the time not being much past the '¡Hola!' and ordering a *cerveza* stage.

"Can we stay on the site?" I tried. "Is it open?"

"Oh sure," was the answer.

He took out his mobile phone and spoke to someone.

"It's OK is it?" I asked hopefully.

Since his reply was in rapid Spanish, I had to resort to my Spanish dictionary in the hope of making some sense of what he'd just said.

"*Se puede?*" He took it off of me and searched for a word. The English translation of the word he pointed to was *girlfriend*.

"Your girlfriend will come to check us in?"

"Si señora. Find place. You stay. Will be here later."

So his girlfriend would be along later to book us in. Fine. We'd already found a place we wanted to stop on between the 'permanents', and soon were established for the night.

When a tall and handsome young black man turned up at our door a little later talking Spanish, the only word of which we understood to be "passport", we took him to be a fellow traveller enquiring where the office was to take it to. The expected *señorita* still hadn't turned up to register us and collect the site fee so we tried to explain what we thought was going on.

"Someone will be along later to sort things out," I ventured, trying not to raise my voice in the English-speaking-to-foreigner manner, and illustrating my words with a few appropriate arm gestures.

Not surprisingly, he seemed baffled, but we were determined to be friendly, and I asked where he was from etc, at last getting my money's worth from the Spanish language classes I'd taken. He must have thought we were real fruit-cakes, because eventually he gave up, shook his head, and in true Continental fashion, shrugged his shoulders and left.

As I'd still not recovered my nerves entirely from the anxieties of that day's journey with its fruitless campsite pursuits and low underpasses, it was easy to see why my imagination then decided to go *off on one*. Somewhere at the back of my mind I began to recall tabloid scare stories about unsuspecting tourists being murdered for their passports. We were in the perfect situation for the same thing to happen to us. After all, there was no record yet of us being on this site, nobody else appeared to be staying there, and our visitor seemed a bit too interested in passports than was healthy. I voiced these alarming thoughts to Harry.

"I'm sure I heard something about this – tourists being killed for their passports. People on their own, people on the road!"

"Oh for goodness sake, it's fine here. Don't worry!"

But I could see that I'd planted a seed of doubt even in *his* sensible mind as he eyed the large claw hammer he kept inside the cab as insurance. This did nothing for my peace of mind; my heart began to thump and I went weak at the knees. Who would know we were there? We wouldn't be missed for ages. We were a gift for criminals.

"You'll feel better after a nice meal and a couple of glasses of wine," he tried to reassure me yet again. "I'll cook."

With my stomach doing somersaults, eating was the last thing I wanted to do – apart from wave a magic wand and be whisked back to the safety of England. I did manage all the wine and a *morsel* of food however, and after clearing everything away, we decided to take a walk around the camp in an effort to take my mind off of things rather than sit in the van awaiting our fate. Unfortunately this had the opposite effect. My fears were reinforced by the god-forsaken nature of the place and the fast-disappearing light, and even my long-suffering husband may have been spooked in the process. Weighing up the situation, we thought we could always leave, but there was no other site close by. After all, we were 'lucky' to find this one, and in the dark the thought of wild camping was even worse to me than our present situation, however terrifying I'd built it up to be. As far as I was concerned, 'wild campers' would be the ideal targets for these passport-stealing, tourist-murdering desperados.

Nearing the relative safety of our van once more, imperceptibly at first, a familiar sound began to drift across the warm Spanish twilight: the soft and distinct singing voice of Rastafarian icon and all-round good guy, Bob Marley.

"*No woman, no cry!*" he sang reassuringly.

It was a rare thing to hear music on the *Costas* which neither contained the manic beat of flamenco nor the mind-numbing thud of disco. Almost miraculous as far as I was concerned.

Seeking out the source of this sweet sound, we rounded a corner and there he was chilling out in the doorway of a small wooden chalet. Not the Jamaican singer himself of course, although we could see his familiar black and white image on a poster inside, but our young passport obsessed visitor. If this had been a cartoon, the bubble over our heads would have contained a large light bulb. He was in charge of the camp during the low season and not the workman's mysterious girlfriend - as far as we knew.

"I should ditch that useless bloody dictionary," was one of my first thoughts on the matter.

Both of us waved casually, calling out "¡*Hola!*" with as much nonchalance as we could muster. I felt really bad about thinking him to be some kind of criminal. He seemed pleased to have some company and it didn't take long to discover that his first language was French, the only language I don't feel too much of a fool using, apart of course from English. Though sometimes even that is in doubt. All the previous confusion could now be sorted out.

"We thought you wanted to stay here," I admitted, "you were asking about passports!"

He laughed heartily at the misunderstanding.

We apologised profusely and arranged to pay at the office the following day.

"Oh and of course we'll bring our passports!"

"We love Bob Marley," I told him. I loved him even more that night.

To say I was walking on air with relief as we said our *Bonsoirs* that night would be an understatement, but all this worry only served to reinforce the fact that I was definitely not cut out for our modest adventure. To have a good imagination is fine when you want to write a novel, but I was beginning to think that without mine I'd have a much better time.

During our travels, I formulated this little piece of philosophy. Brits travelling around Europe in Springtime are at a big disadvantage. Experience tells us that a few days of sunshine in April could be the only decent spell of weather until September, so as soon as we lose that extra hour heralding lighter evenings, all sense of decency is relinquished. Sane individuals begin appearing in *public* wearing shorts and sandals despite the North wind, and our beaches are littered with optimistically goose-pimpled sun-worshippers.

Those living in more felicitous climates, such as the Spanish and Italians, refuse to concede that summer has arrived until the local temperature is at least into the high 80s.

A scene on the local bus in the Spanish city of Segovia during early June was enough to confirm this theory. I noticed that fellow passengers, mainly school children and ancient ladies, were all bundled up in sweaters and winter coats. I felt daringly under-dressed in my flimsy summer dress and sandals. As a further precaution to catching a chill, the schoolgirls also wore thick woolly tights. Just looking at them made me feel like fainting.

UNEASY RIDER

While we were in Italy, the locals didn't deem it worth opening their outdoor swimming pools until halfway through July. By this time, we thought the risk of hypothermia might be reduced ever so slightly by temperatures well into the upper 70s Fahrenheit, but we were alone in this. Once the thermometer reached 90 degrees though, they seemed to decide that yes, it might be possible to leave the *Versace* overcoats at home, and flocked like lemmings to the nearest lido. Here they threw caution to the wind along with most of their clothes, and proceeded to fry themselves on sun-beds. Much better to risk a melanoma than a chill, surely. In England it would only take a couple of days of temperatures above average to find the tabloids plastered with *"Phwoar, what a scorcher!"* type headlines, accompanied by the usual tacky photo's of bikini-clad young women cavorting in Hyde Park. But I suppose those Italians are at least sure that once summer starts, they will actually get one.

These conflicting ideas of what constitutes a hot day led to disappointment on so many occasions. After being cooped up for miles in the un-airconditioned van, often only the thought of plunging into the pool at the next campsite kept the spirits up and stopped us from disintegrating into a bad-tempered, frazzled heap. It was slightly annoying therefore to find the advertised pool empty. Empty that is apart from a Coke can and the inevitable puddle of what you can only hope is merely dirty yellow rainwater rather than something even less desirable.

There was occasionally a dubious advantage in being too early for our 'summer' pursuits. When we were well in 'advance' of what the Southern Europeans deem to be the holiday season, actually as late as the end of May, we stayed for free on several unmanned and deserted French 'municipal' sites. Unfortunately the cheapness of our stay on these places was far outweighed by my feeling that as the sole occupants, we were vulnerable to all those nasty murderers and robbers taking refuge in the equally deserted-looking local village.

In the end, it made no difference to me that we'd paid for our night on the site in *Puzol*. Feeling safe anywhere without bricks and mortar is about as unlikely for me as … well the UK winning the *Eurovision Song Contest* again.

The Parable of a Parador
No Pasarán!

Harry turned off the engine, thumped the steering wheel of the campervan and shouted,

"You wanted to come here. You get us out of it!"

My stomach was gripped with that sickening feeling of panic and as I tried desperately to hold back the tears. As a thousand tiny needles pricked my eyes, the saying, *"Beware of what you wish for, it may come true"* began to echo though my mind in an annoyingly smug way. To stay in the *Parador* of *Arcos de la Frontera* had been my wish. Now it was a dream turning into a nightmare.

My fateful discovery of the Parador happened during a language class at our local college. Little did I know, as the tutor put the video in the slot, that my life would soon change forever. Well, a slight exaggeration, but I did become rather obsessive. The innocent scene on the screen unfolded in an effort to teach would-be tourists to ask if it was *possible* to do something - *"Se puede…*

The scene:

*… A couple sit on the terrace of the Parador at Arcos de la Frontera, perusing their guidebooks. A waiter arrives, obviously the genuine article since he looks somewhat ill at ease in front of the camera. They ask him if it is possible to have a meal out there… " Se puede…" etc. The answer unfortunately for them, is in the negative, **but** they can have a drink! …*

All of this might sound mundane, but the setting wasn't. The 80s-styled, shoulder-padded *señorita* presenting the video wandered through the shady streets of the town of *Arcos de la Frontera*, one of the 'white towns' or *'pueblos blancos'* of *Andalucia*. These towns are romantically set on top of a hill or a vertiginous cliff-face, and since all of the houses in them are painted white, it does not take a genius to see how they got their name. The Parador of Arcos sits on the summit at the edge of the high outcrop on which the town is situated. From below it seems to be in a precarious position, suspended like an ornament on a Christmas tree. The views in the video, taken from and around this lofty position, were spectacular and I was hooked.

While the possession of a guidebook can give a sense of security in that you think it tells you all you need to know, believe me, this is far from the case. Our Spanish guidebook had a lovely photograph of my imagined utopia, and the caption below the picture calmly stated:

"Precipitously situated Arcos de la Frontera, a challenge to motorists"

"Challenge to motorists?" I thought. "We've driven up and down Swiss mountains for years; this can't be any worse! What kind of wimps do they think we British are? O.K. it looks steep, but nothing we can't cope with, surely?"

However, whenever I use the word, *surely*, at the back of my mind I can hear the lugubrious tone of our history teacher at school. Not the most inspiring of teachers, and also not keen on the exuberance of youth, Mrs. Sacher would become exasperated whenever someone uttered this word, grimly admonishing,

"No-one can ever be that sure about anything!"

Like most things young people are warned about, we took no notice and deliberately used the word just to annoy the poor old thing. But she may have had a point after all.

"We could have a night in a Parador if you like," my considerate Other Half said, "it'll probably make a nice change from being cooped up in the van by then."

I ordered the Parador brochure and eagerly awaited its arrival. My enthusiasm was not curbed by its contents, and even though full of intriguing places such as restored castles, convents and palaces, my heart was set on the former home of the *corrigidor* at Arcos. I had pictured myself gazing out from that terrace, glass of *Rioja* in one hand (although no food). There really was nothing else that could possibly compete.

"Well it just has to be the one at Arcos," I said, showing Harry the brochure.

"If that's what you want, then we'll go for it."

And so it was that a few months later our Spanish sojourn took us *en route* north from Cadiz, seeking out this fabled place like conquistadors on a quest to find *El Dorado*. Or at least a less exciting without-horses version anyway.

Upon arrival outside the town our mission ground to a halt. It was not entirely clear how to get up to our destination or even into the town itself. We could see it so temptingly out of reach at the edge of the cliff above us, and I was reassured to see that it actually resembled the guidebook picture. The endearing Spanish tradition of making strangers guess how to find their way around was in practice, and there were no visible directions to the Parador despite its VHS fame.

"Let's find the Tourist Office," I suggested.

"You'll be lucky. It's bound to be their four-hour *lunch* break," Harry replied.

He was right of course. How many times had we optimistically tried to get information from one of these places only to discover them closed and not only because of *lunch* but also because it was a Saint's Day/Monday/election day/out of season. Perish the thought of a tourist office actually being open when it was needed.

"Well, there's got to be a way up to the Parador, otherwise how would it be in business?"

Harry, resigned to his role as reluctant tour driver, shrugged his shoulders, put the van into gear and we set off once more. The first guess we made as to the way up and into the lower part of town only led to 'no entry' signs. At this point it was a pity we didn't hear the warning bells, though we would hear enough real ones later. Even at this early stage, Harry was uncharacteristically ready to give up.

"Come on. Let's forget about it," he whined.

I was determined not to be deprived of my goal.

"We just can't go away without trying a bit harder," I had after all come so far and got so tantalisingly near.

He resisted. I insisted. He lost, for once.

With each time we drove back and forth across its bridges, the foreign green river flowing at the base of the hill upon which Arcos is so "precipitously" set, soon became as familiar as our local town's supermarket-trolley-containing-stream. However, by the process of elimination, we eventually found a road that thankfully didn't lead us back to where we'd just come from, and I felt that now I could actually look forward to my night of five-star luxury. Things were now looking up both literally and metaphorically as this road was of a reasonable width and actually not too steep. But soon the ominous appearance of one-way signs again tried to confound us, and beads of sweat ran down my forehead, and this time not because of the Spanish heat.

"This is hopeless," it was so unlike my normally confident Other Half to admit defeat.

"It can't be much further!" I said, trying to cover up the fact that I actually agreed with him.

The higher and further into the town we drove, the narrower became the streets. Not in the sense of British narrowness, that is with pavements or verges and the sensible addition of the occasional passing place, but in the sense of those white, unforgiving walls of buildings actually being the sides of the road. In my enthusiasm, it hadn't occurred to me for one second that when donkeys were the only form of transport and in an effort to achieve relief from the relentless summer heat of Southern Spain, houses in towns were built as close together as possible. Our guidebook with its emphasis on the steepness of the streets, had neglectfully omitted to mention their width. And I'd paid good money for it too. There'd been no warning signs. There was no room for manoeuvre. Any possibility of turning round was a non-starter, and in any case out of necessity this was a one-way system.

Just as we thought things couldn't get worse, they did. A low archway loomed ahead of us, making the way forward even narrower than before. We were stuck. Backing up was out of the question because since we'd stopped, the world of Arcos and its wife had decided to take a spin in the car and a queue had built in our wake. With both sides of the van threatening to add a new dimension to the walls of the houses, it was nigh on impossible for either of us even to climb out. That we might actually be in a tricky situation did seem a big possibility. On the plus side however, like Pollyanna I'd found a silver lining.

"Look! There's a sign for the Parador! Over on that wall!"

Our enforced stop had enabled me to spot the small sign pointing up yet another steep and narrow turning beyond the archway. The usually unflappable Harry was already disenchanted with the trip in general and with Spain in particular. This was proving to be the last straw on top the huge stack we'd accumulated since leaving home two weeks before.

"Well in the first place, I doubt if we can get through the arch – and anyway, how do you think I can get the van round that corner? This van's got a long wheelbase – there's no chance!"

Now was the time for him to succumb to that uncharacteristic bout of steering wheel thumping and towel-throwing-in. Helpfully I just shut my eyes and wished I could curl up in a ball and die.

Then, through the murky depths of our despair an apparition appeared before us in the shape of a young man on a motor scooter waving his arms about.

"I think he's trying to help," I said realising that he wasn't just making rude gestures at hapless tourists (us).

With no other options, Harry had to go along with it.

"Well it looks like he's hinting we should pull the wing mirrors in."

It seemed a sensible suggestion and one worth trying even though we were unsure if this would completely solve our predicament. By now we were also becoming aware that we'd attracted the interest of several ancient and well-oiled patrons of a bar just up ahead, and our little drama turned into a full-scale pantomime as they began gesticulating and beckoning us on.

"*Si! Si! ... Se puede!*" they exclaimed excitedly and at the same time doing what could only be described as some sort of grotesque ritual dance.

This was a good time to remember the meaning of those words in my favourite scene from the language video.

"*Se Puede*! **They** seem to think we can do it!" I translated helpfully.

It was not like Harry to give up, but the high temperatures and a general fatigue which we were both feeling as a result of driving hundreds of miles since leaving home had taken their toll. After all, being from an island which is only some 22 ½ miles at its widest[1] the distances involved in our ambitious circumnavigation of Spain were by comparison, not even a ball-game let alone a different one. I don't really think the re-spray carried out on the van as part of its re-fit before we left home had anything to do with his sudden caution, but no doubt the thought of that new paintwork being given the *sgraffito* treatment didn't help. Paintwork aside, there was no real choice for a way out of our situation. The only alternative to cutting the van up into small pieces and carting it off to one of the charming scrap heaps we'd noticed enhancing the *Andalucían* countryside, was to trust these helpful locals who were *surely* experienced in this type of thing. Slightly encouraged by the sight of a small local bus (wing mirrors folded of course) behind us, though not quite as large as our van, we edged forwards.

"If that goes through every day, then *surely* we can!" Pollyanna chirped.

Of course we had no reason to know that the bus did not actually include a stop up that hill and outside 'our' Parador, but emboldened by its presence, Harry managed to squeeze the van through the archway. Now all that was needed was to get it round that wretched tight corner beyond, which was so tantalisingly displaying the sign to the object of my desire. Inch by inch, Harry shunted the van backwards and forwards until eventually we found ourselves liberated in the wide expanses of the town *plaza mayor*. There stood my Parador occupying the whole of one side of the square, white and shiny, the jewel in the crown. On one of the other sides was a picturesquely-crumbling Baroque church and a third consisted of the vertiginous cliff-edge with its breath-taking views of the surrounding parched countryside. How wonderful, how authentic. At last, the real Spain! The Spain of Laurie Lee... the country as I had imagined it to be when my hero walked across it in those far off days…

I soon had to come back to the here and now because our next difficulty was finding somewhere to leave the van. The square, rather than being an open space for the recreation of the good people of Arcos, was a car park. It was at this point that something important occurred to Harry.

"You should have booked a room. After all this trouble, we might not be able to stay there anyway. You didn't think of that did you?"

Why was it always my fault? But I couldn't argue. It *was* my idea to stay in the place, as he'd already so forcibly reminded me.

"You'd better get in there! Here's the Traffic Warden wanting to move us on!"

A mean-looking uniformed man was heading our way, so I willingly left Harry to sort out the problem of parking, and jumped out of the van to make a dash for the hotel reception. It was only then I realised that I looked like a disaster area. My hair was all over the place from travelling with the van windows open, and I was wearing the faded-tee-shirt-shorts-and-flip-flops look that had been great for dossing around on campsites, but to not really suitable attire for a five-star hotel. For the first time in my sheltered life I needed to stop being squeamish about my appearance. I was already unpopular for bringing us here, so it was no good whinging that I should change into something more respectable - or at least put a comb through my hair. Paraphrasing in my mind the words of *Basil Fawlty*, *"Only the upper classes would wear tat like that"*, I hoped the hotel staff would think me one of those English eccentrics, as was our erstwhile reputation abroad before the arrival of the package holiday and the lager lout.

As I neared the entrance, I noticed a smartly dressed couple making their way up the steep path to the hotel pulling suitcases behind them. Of course, unlike us, they were hardly likely to have trundled all that way up to the Parador without booking, but with no time to apply this bit of logic to the situation, I found myself running the last few yards to bag the imagined last room in the place. Obviously used to all sorts there, nobody at the reception desk batted an eyelid at my accelerated arrival technique and bohemian appearance. I just couldn't go back to Harry without the key to a room. My heart was in my mouth making speech difficult as I enquired calmly if they had a room available, and for once it was a joy to fill in the annoying forms in exchange for the key. I returned to the van in triumph. It was a pleasant surprise to discover that the parking man was not mean at all, and was directing Harry to a suitable vacant space in the square. I couldn't help thinking though that any change of attitude may have been our elevated status as guests in the *Parador* rather than ageing hippies in a scruffy camper van.

After all the stress, we were keen to get out of the suffocating heat of that town square, multiplied a hundred–fold inside our tin-box of a home. We grabbed what we needed for that night, including our 'posh' clothes, and stuffed everything apart from these into a small case. I'd insisted on bringing this with us for such an occasion, despite being told there was no space for such frivolities.

"What's wrong with using carrier bags?" I'd been asked.

"Well if you don't know, I can't be bothered to tell you." It was against my principles to enter my precious Parador like a couple of bag-ladies.

We made our way up to the room and I gasped as we entered. It was huge, with its own entrance hall, comfy sofas, tables and chairs. It was heaven.

"Let's just stay here for the next week, abandon the van and fly home," I suggested.

"Well don't forget whose idea it was to do this trip in the first place, and you hate flying!"

The bathroom alone could have accommodated the living space inside the campervan some four times over. A lifetime had passed since I'd been able to wallow in a deep bathful of warm water. Designers of campsite showers needed to go back to the drawing board. Nine times out of ten my clothes managed to get as wet as I did, and it was normal for water not to be as hot as advertised on the tap. Not unusual either was that this so-called 'hot' water ran out half way through washing my hair resulting in a lot of futile insults being shouted at the pipe-work. I wasn't used to roughing it and this was not my idea of a good time.

Before we could begin to enjoy our surroundings properly, we had to undertake the important task of transferring our cheese supply and other perishables from the van 'fridge into the chilled mini bar in the room. The refrigeration facilities in the van were just about adequate whilst on the move, though good when plugged into the mains on a campsite, but obviously no such arrangements were available in that scorching Town Square.

Having done the deed, we could now turn our attention to enjoying the view from our balcony. It was an excellent vantage point for observing the comings and goings in the *plaza* below. A good source of interest came from the police station on the opposite side to the Parador. From our observations, the *guardia* of Arcos may have the best policing job in the world. Their main duties seemed to consist of:

a) Lounging provocatively, James Dean-like, astride large motor bikes

b) Smoking huge cigars

c) Chatting to and sharing a joke with various passing acquaintances

Along with peaked caps, sun-glasses and large moustaches seemed to be obligatory parts of their uniform, so when a workman wearing a yellow hard-hat stopped for a chat, the ensemble was in danger of resembling the *'Village People'*. The temptation for a chorus of *'Y.M.C.A.'* was too much to resist.

The superfluous number of police in that square didn't seem to have much to do. We thought that film careers may have beckoned if *The Italian Job* transferred to Arcos from Turin and with motorbikes rather than Minis. Those narrow, steep and winding alleyways would certainly make it an exciting prospect – maybe we should suggest it to someone.

However, pleasant as this was and not wishing to spend the whole time in Arcos playing the voyeur, we ventured out into the square. The tourist office (yes, there was one all the way up there) was next to the police station, but I was left wondering if it might have been better located somewhere near the town's entrance for visitors to take full advantage. Anyone who had already made it up to the *plaza major* would probably have no need for one by then. On the door was a poster advertising guided walking tours of the town's historic buildings and apparently famous *patios*. Naturally it did not re-open until later that afternoon, so as temperatures began to cool, we returned and took up the offer. As a bonus, this was free for guests of the Parador. Being the only interested party that day, we had an exclusive tour with the pleasant raven-haired young woman from the tourist office, who spoke impeccable English. Harry even managed to make her laugh, something of a feat in Spain, as we passed a noisy bunch of Germans intent on disrupting the tranquillity of those narrow streets:

"Tut, tourists!" he said, "We get them at home!"

Despite seeing the exquisite patios and learning the interesting history of the town, I began to feel uneasy. The recurrent pealing of bells from its many church *campanile* along with chiming clocks, reminded me that one side of the square containing the Parador was taken up by that ancient church. Churches mean bells; bells mean laying awake half the night. This had been an enduring memory from a previous trip through the Spanish Pyrenees, where clocks chimed not only on the hour, but five minutes before and after. This helpfully made sure that listeners just dropping back to sleep after the first lot were in no doubt of the time for the rest of the night.

"Those bells," I wondered. "They must stop at night, mustn't they?"

"I expect so," was Harry's unconvincing answer.

I put the thought to the back of my mind. We were here and it was all going to be fantastic.

During this tour of the town, like a recurring nightmare an old worry again reared its ugly head. If it was difficult getting up to the top of the place, what would the journey down be like? Deciding to investigate the route we'd have to take the next day, it did nothing to reassure us. If anything, the streets were narrower and had more bends even sharper than those we'd negotiated on the way up. Optimist was now my middle name.

"There's no point in worrying about it now. It can't be that bad. That bus must use the road, after all."

I was trying to play it down, but Harry was in no mood to be buoyed up by false cheerfulness.

"It's definitely much worse than the way up," he said, "and that bus was smaller than us anyway – it had a much shorter wheel-base!"

"I wish you'd stop going on about wheel-bases and cheer up a bit," but I kept this thought to myself. I seemed to have stolen his middle name and this defeatist attitude was becoming a habit.

There was no point though in letting the possible troubles of the morrow ruin the rest of our stay in *Arcos*, so we returned to the Parador and the luxury of being able to stretch out in that lovely bath and move around the room without treading on each other's feet. Our evening in the Parador of *Arcos de la Frontera* was perfect. We ate a wonderful evening meal in the restaurant where smiling waitresses were charmingly dressed in traditional brightly-coloured Adalucian costume. They thoughtfully brought us extra supplies of the giant *tapas* olives after noticing we'd polished off the first bowl in seconds, and didn't blanche for one moment when we requested a vegetarian meal. Nothing was too much trouble, and everything was accompanied by an old-fashioned serving of helpfulness.

That college video hadn't deceived me about the incredible view from the Parador. Our dining room vantage point was above scores of swallows and bats swooping and screeching around the cliffs below in the twilight - a magical experience that almost compensated for all the tiring difficulties and inconveniences of the previous weeks of travelling.

"Well it is an amazing view," Harry had to admit, "Now we're here, perhaps we can forget about staying in a parador for the foreseeable future!"

Had I gone on about it that much? Well, I guess I had.

Afterwards, we stood on the terrace overlooking both the plaza and the surrounding landscape. A million stars twinkled in an endless sky unpolluted by light. No sound of traffic broke the tranquillity. The air was balmy and perfumed with the herbs of the sierra that stretched out into misty blue folds towards the horizon. I breathed in deeply and knew I would always remember this perfect moment in such a perfect place. I did not want it to end. I was actually staying in the Parador at Arcos, and could not believe how lovely it all was. Then an unwelcome but familiar sound began to invade my euphoria…the bells!

We returned to our room and reassured ourselves that more than likely they would cease at midnight. After all, the *powers-that-be* whoever they were, wouldn't want to upset their paying guests in the Parador. We were deluding ourselves. The various bells of *Arcos* did not take a rest and were determined to deprive us of ours. Along with striking each quarter, the clock in that picturesque church tower marked each hour with a tune that seemed so quaint and pretty in daylight hours. Throughout that hot, interminable night it became a thing of torment. And as if that wasn't enough, for good measure we were treated to an extra peal for matins at some unearthly hour while it was still dark outside. Once this was over, it was then that the local dustcart arrived. Not noted anywhere in the world as being a quiet activity, the garbage collection in the *plaza mayor* of *Arcos de la Frontera* was no exception. How anyone got any sleep in that place I'll never know.

By the morning we were completely shattered and did not relish the drive back down from the town. Harry always thought things through.

"If we leave it till everyone's having their siesta this afternoon, we might have more room to manoeuvre, and you can do a bit more exploring if you want."

There were a lot of fascinating nooks and crannies I'd noticed during our guided tour of the previous evening, so this seemed like an excellent scheme. I didn't think Harry would want to darken the doors of *Arcos de la Frontera* ever again.

Arcos really is a stunning place, but all too soon we realised we couldn't put off taking our leave any longer. In my new-found rôle of tour optimist, I had a bright idea which I hoped might help with the drive down.

"Why don't I walk in front of the van to see how much room we have each side?"

We'd only be going at a snail's pace, so it seemed a sensible thing to do.

"Well, I suppose you could try it," was Harry's over-enthusiastic reply.

"I could carry a red flag! You know, like they used to when cars first went on roads."

"Mmm. Well let's just get going." My suggestion had fallen flat on its face.

Like a pathetically small carnival procession though without the music, singing and dancing (in fact nothing like a carnival procession come to think of it), we made our tentative way along, Harry in campervan behind, me in front but minus the red flag. As we feared though, the way down was even more torturous and problematic than the way up and our hope that there would be no other cars on the road at that time proved to be just that. Almost immediately we 'picked up' a rearguard intent on staying as close to us as a Garfield on a rear windscreen and our polite pleas for him to back up and allow us a bit of space were unsympathetically ignored. So again we had little room to manoeuvre at each bend.

After what felt like eternity, we reached the wider expanses of the road leading out of *Arcos*. I'd done my best to gauge the clearances, but it obviously wasn't good enough seeing as in places our van's smart new paintwork now looked like it had been set upon by

Jackson Pollock with a pen-knife. Along one side a nasty dent had appeared to balance the composition. We were free though, *relatively* unscathed and the ordeal of that suffocating afternoon at least was at an end.

Harry pulled over and stopped. He was looking not a little wearied by all the strenuous wheel-turning and shunting backwards and forwards, and sunk the most-part of a large bottle of water. If we hadn't planned to drive on to Seville that day, the occasion would have called for something a bit stronger. I was keen to get going again, but he had other ideas.

"Let's just sit here for a while," he murmured, closing his eyes to end any possibility of discussion on the subject.

We sat quietly and enjoyed the feeling of liberation.

"Thank goodness we don't have to do that again!" I was good at stating the bleeding obvious.

At the time we were not quite ready to find anything actually funny about our experience, but I couldn't stop myself laughing hysterically with relief.

A few days later, when all of this was becoming a distant memory to be reeled out as one of our 'adventures' when we got home, we had arrived in Seville. Stopping for diesel on the outskirts of the city, I found myself amusing the friendly service station attendant there.

He pointed to the obviously fresh damage,

"What ees? You have bang?"

Without thinking, I began to paraphrase the slogan used by the Republican faction in the Spanish Civil War, which was quoted prominently in the film, *'Land and Freedom'*. I pointed to the scrapes and said with feeling,

"*Arcos de la Frontera. No Pasarán!*" (None shall pass!)

"Ah, Si! Si!" he laughed, appreciating the joke.

As soon as I'd said it though, I felt certain I'd committed an awful *faux pas*. Was it in good taste to make light of what was, after all, still a sensitive part of Spanish history? I'm still not certain, but unlike *Mr Fawlty*, I mentioned the war and I think I really did get away with it.

Had our visit to *Arcos de la Frontera* been worth all of that hassle? I shall always treasure the memory of that magical moment on the terrace of the Parador. There will be no room for such romantic notions in Harry's mind though. It will evermore be the place where we acquired that dent in the van and which, during the rest of the time we owned the vehicle and despite all his efforts to eliminate it, still continued to serve as a constant reminder:

It is not always a good thing to have a wish fulfilled.

And I'm sad to say we never did sit on the Parador's sunny terrace and have that glass of Rioja!

Note (1) Namely the Isle of Wight

Inauguration of the Innocent
Absolute Beginners

We stood amidst the chaos and all agreed that we'd probably made a big mistake. Two weeks of this. Still, there was nothing we could do but make the best of it that night. For an unfortunate moment, I found myself quoting Scarlett O'Hara.

"Well after all, tomorrow is another day!" No-one was in the mood to laugh.

Things would surely look better in the morning. They couldn't look much worse.

This chaotic beginning to our first time out in a camper van could have put us off for life. We'd left it a bit late really. Our two children were leggy teenagers, and the thought of being seen in such an uncool thing as a camper van that was not a VW had been embarrassing in the extreme. They'd needed persuading to come on the trip in the first place. I felt so despondent that first night, I could have wept with the hopelessness of it all and just wished Scotty could simply beam us up to boldly go back to the comfort of our own home. A fortnight in the thing seemed to loom before us like a 'lifer's' prison sentence.

You may be wondering exactly how we got ourselves into this mess ...

We were all sitting round the table, mellowed with a meal and a glass of wine, when my Other Half Harry, made a suggestion for that year's summer holiday.

"Why don't we hire a camper van and do that trip down through France to Spain you've always talked about? It'll be great!"

Well, I'd always wanted to find out why my hero, Laurie Lee had loved Spain.

Our dear offspring groaned.

"No, 'cos that would be **too** embarrassing," our 16 year-old daughter said helpfully.

"Well who's going to see you in it in France?"

"French people?" This was difficult to deny.

"Well it might be a laugh," our 18 year-old son had begun to warm to the idea.

We should have realised that taking a camper van off of the Island would be a great deal more involved than throwing a couple of suitcases into the *Saab* boot and heading for the ferry, but that night we were too taken up with the idea for such minor details.

Harry visited the local Motor-Home hirers next day and we began to make plans. Having to load the van in less than half an hour had not featured in the original plan though: once we'd booked both Isle of Wight and Cross-Channel ferries, we discovered that the earliest time we could collect the van from the hirer's was just an hour before our booking on the former. We couldn't catch the next one, as this was the latest that would connect with the Cross Channel service. On top of this, vehicles are meant to arrive at both ferry terminals at least half an hour before departure.

"It'll be fine," my optimistic husband reassured me as I started to have my doubts. "You can have everything ready and waiting. There are four of us to get all the stuff loaded after all."

When I consider now that in later years I could easily spend a leisurely week loading our own van just for the two of us, I'm amazed that we even attempted to do it in such a short amount of time. But we were so innocent then.

If you've never lived on an island, it may seem idyllic but you just cannot appreciate the inconvenience involved. The Isle of

Wight does have advantages, but these are vastly outweighed by all that is involved in getting off of it. One of the results of this is that all the best young brains leave with their owners for mainland Universities and rarely come back for anything other than a cheap holiday with their parents. Another is this. If you want to travel to France, you have to get off of the Island first. In the height of summer it can require the skills of a military logistics team to work out the timing of it all.

The day for the 'off' came all too soon. Apart from putting food and other useful items into boxes awaiting Harry and son to arrive with our temporary home, my job was to sort out the problem of how to transfer the clothes from house to van quickly. My usually wise husband made a suggestion,

"Just leave them in the hall. We can all grab a pile,"

This was not my preferred method,

"Well I'm not having everything I've spent ages ironing getting screwed up! I can pack everything in the cases and offload them into the cupboards in the van. Then just chuck the cases back into the house."

What could be simpler?

Since thinking things through is not my forté, that this would all take time hadn't crossed my mind. Time was the thing we didn't have and neither did we have a previous knowledge of the internal layout of the motor caravan we were hiring.

Once the van arrived, it didn't take long for my so-called organisation to disappear into a cloud of panic. We had no time to search out all those cunningly concealed stowage places, and each case had its neatly folded contents tipped out unceremoniously onto the van seats. One case however ended up being strapped onto the roof, but this did in fact come in handy later for solving the problem of storing dirty washing. There was even a flaw in this otherwise inspired solution though. A week later, following a downpour in the Pyrenees, the dampened towels inside this case fermented nicely in the August heat of Southern France. They were never quite the same again.

Somehow however, we did manage to get everything into our little temporary home and miraculously arrived in time for the Solent ferry we were booked on. Being a Saturday in the height of the holiday season though, meant that the service was running behind schedule. Normally this would have been a good thing for last-minuters like us, but only if we didn't have to catch another boat on the other side.

As we sat in our still-frenzied state on the slipway waiting to be directed onto the car deck, one of the loading operators approached.

"Can you wait for the next one mate?" he asked Harry, "You should've gone on first and I'm not sure if we can fit you in at the back…"

Being a high vehicle, the van wouldn't fit under the raised deck at the centre of the boat. I had to admire Harry's calmness:

"Sorry mate," he replied casually, "We've got to catch the Cross Channel ferry."

"OK. I'll try to get you on," said our new best friend.

Unlike me, Harry knew that the polite approach always gets the best results, even if below the surface you feel like screaming.

Despite the delay, we were relieved to reach Portsmouth and the Brittany Ferries terminal with at least a few minutes to spare.

"You've cut it a bit fine!" shouted Jobsworth at the entrance to the car deck.

I felt like saying, "Well have you shut the doors? Has the boat left?" But of course I didn't want us to get thrown off for abusing staff, so kept quiet.

He'd obviously taken a course on stating the bleeding obvious and we *were* almost half an hour later than we should have been.

"People don't realise what a pain that bit of water is," I mused.

But as I said before, only we Island dwellers can appreciate this.

Once safely onto the car deck, we had time to survey the disaster area which was the inside of the van. With tins and packets carpeting the floor, the central aisle resembled a supermarket visited by looters. It was hard to tell where the floor ended and where the seats began. All the clothes that I'd meticulously ironed and folded prior to our departure were now piles of jumble sale leftovers. I began to doubt whether we would ever find anything again. Even though the five hours spent sailing across to France could have been put to good use at that moment, as passengers aren't allowed on the car deck during the crossing, we had to sit it out trying not to think about the chaos waiting for us below.

Our first night on a campsite near *Caen* had already been booked through the ferry company, which was just as well, since it was getting late and already dark by the time we reached the shores of France. At least we knew where we were heading for and finding it was easy, though I had the feeling that this was not through my excellent map-reading skills. In theory, being on the main road meant that we couldn't go far wrong. Since this was August though, by the time we arrived, the place was heaving with French holiday-makers and as we drove round the site, it seemed that a Continental free-for-all system of pitch reservation was in operation. The only pitch left appeared to be a very narrow one between two high hedges. Great for privacy, but not the easiest thing to reverse into in an unfamiliarly large vehicle, in the dark. Still, we were safely placed for the night, though our difficulties of that day were yet to be ended. Harry sorted out the cable to plug us, or rather the van, into the mains.

"I just don't believe it!" he groaned.

"Now what?"

"We've got the wrong connector."

My heart sunk.

"Mr - assured me that it had the Continental adapter fitted!" Harry groaned. Thrashing about in the dark in a bid to 'get sorted', was the last thing we needed, but I had every confidence in my Other Half. Prepared for most emergencies, my hero calmly remedied the situation with the deft use of a screwdriver, and we had light. What we needed next was food and sleep.

A bowl of tinned soup and some home-bought rolls had to suffice for dinner that night, but this was as welcome as any gourmet feast after our long day. Somehow toothbrushes, night clothes and bedding for everyone were extracted from amongst those piles of worldly goods. The seating rearranged into beds and also turned out to conceal the previously longed-for storage spaces underneath. Everything not needed that night was shoved into these. If only we'd known they were there in the first place. Our bed did not need to be fashioned from seats because it was tucked up above the driver's 'cab'. The drawback to this arrangement however was that because of a combination of short legs and a lack of acrobatic skills, each night we were away I provided an entertaining cabaret act for the rest of the family. My attempts to climb up and into this confined space was not helped by being subjected to hysterical laughter from the rest of the family, and then succumbing to it myself. The same performance was repeated in reverse each morning, although gravity did help a bit in this instance. However, needing to use *the facilities* in the night was the worst part of this arrangement. I firstly had to climb over Harry without poking an elbow in his face and then disembark from our 'shelf' without making any noise – about as possible as eating a packet of crisps quietly.

The next day began bright and clear, and following such a fraught beginning we were all surprisingly keen to get going and make the most of our trip. First though, I insisted that we undertake an hilarious activity which came to resemble something from *'The Generation Game'*. Matching the right clothes to the right person from the bundles so hastily shoved under the seats the night before was not as easy as it sounds. For instance, I seemed to be the only one who knew whose socks were whose. In other words, which belonged to our son and which to his dad.

"I'm not wearing HIS socks!"

They recoiled at the thought of wearing each other's even though they were all perfectly clean.

"Socks are socks," I tried telling them, but they weren't having any of it. Men!

Luckily our daughter being a teenager had a more frivolous line in underwear than I, so in fairness, our task was a little easier. Eventually, and like a celeb at a prize-giving, I presented everyone with their reward – a personalised plastic bag of underwear.

As the holiday wore on, everything eventually slotted into place, but even so it was amazing how easy it was to lose something in such a small and confined space. The frantic search we had to find the return Channel ferry tickets when we arrived back at the terminal two weeks later, was a classic example of this.

"I'm sure you said you'd put them somewhere safe!"

"Well **you** must have moved them if I did!"

With everyone trying to prove their innocence, it would have taken a *Hercule Poirot* to find out who actually did the deed. As you can imagine, this did not create the best of atmospheres to end our holiday with.

"So much for our leisurely breakfast," I said.

"Well you should have remembered where **you** put the tickets then!"

I'd been looking forward to freshly brewed coffee and croissants straight from the oven. Instead, we spent most of the time flapping about like headless chickens trying to find those damn tickets. Of course they were eventually discovered in such a safe place, even the most diligent customs officer would have been hard put to find them. And of course everyone denied putting them there in the first place.

The ironic thing was that when we'd arrived there in the early hours of that morning, we felt quite superior to those poor mortals cooped up alongside us in their cars. In previous years we'd also either driven through the night in order to catch the first ferry of the day, or stayed cooped up in our car at the terminal overnight. It was miserable being cramped like sardines, sleeping fitfully, longing for that first sign of the cold grey dawn. On one occasion I even saw a girl had resorted to sleeping on the cold tarmac next to the family car. We'd gazed up at those lucky people relaxing in campervans with all their mod cons. Unlike us though, no doubt none of them had mislaid their tickets.

Despite the unpromising start to this first time away in a van, we realised that the advantages of this mode of travel probably just about outweighed the disadvantages. We saw places that would otherwise have taken years of separate trips to visit when having to return to rented accommodation or hotel rooms each night. Rather than the restrictions of hotel dining hours, we could eat wherever and at whatever time we chose, and if we didn't like a place, we just moved on.

There-again, there was usually nothing to stop us staying on for a few days at somewhere we really liked, and on discovering a fantastic view, it was easy to arrange to have our lunch or tea break over-looking it. If the weather was awful, we could always drive further on in the hope of finding somewhere dry, although the rain sometimes chose to follow us. Also, and maybe most importantly, it was an advantage not having to seek out *public conveniences,* which are things of great rarity in most places. Even when there is one, it often turns out to be a hole in the ground.

Flying directly into an airport or whizzing down a motorway are undoubtedly the quickest ways to get anywhere, but the smaller, quiet roads are far more rewarding. From the high vantage point of a camper van, hedges give up their views and walls their secret gardens beyond.

Of course, disadvantages included being at the mercy of gnats, having to make up beds every night, and worrying if the 'fridge could be kept cold enough to stop the cheese making the place smell like something had died. Another problem was that even though the van may be of a reasonable size, sometimes the type of place we could drive to was restricted: narrow lanes in both countryside and town, along with hilltop villages were difficult. But taking the local bus from campsite to city centre rather than having to find somewhere to park once there was liberating, and having to walk a bit further to your destination often had its own rewards.

Some ten years later when just the two of us set out on the first trip abroad in our own van, we tied it in with a family celebration in a seaside town on the mainland. We could spend the night in it after the party, parked on my parent's drive. Not only would this free-up bed space for other party guests, but would also be a good, although belated chance to try out our new sleeping arrangements in familiar surroundings. The family gathered round to inspect our holiday accommodation, and my younger brother was particularly taken with it.

The party finished late, but as our booking on the Channel Tunnel wasn't until the afternoon on the following day, we planned to have a lay-in. What we didn't plan was to be woken up at the crack of dawn by the New Zealand All-Blacks practising their *Haka* on the van roof.

"What the hell…?"

Harry slid open one of the side windows.

"I'll kill your brother," he murmured.

As the startled gulls flew off screeching as only they can, the crusts of bread that my thoughtful younger sibling had provided for their breakfast was scattered far and wide. It was just the sort of thing he'd do. We saw the funny side eventually, but luckily we couldn't see the mess they had left behind on our newly re-sprayed roof…

On How to Find ... a Campsite

Take my word for it. If you ever need to ask directions in a foreign country, never ask a group of middle-aged women out for their evening *paseo*.

Our first trip away in the Leyland Daf, saw us circumnavigating Spain. Even though I'd obtained a *Mapa de Campings* from the Iberian tourist board before we left home, we soon discovered that there may be sites indicated on this magnificent publication, but with no information on how to find them apart from a 'phone number, it was not much use. Still, it **was** free. With my rudimentary language skills, I wasn't prepared to have a confusing conversation with a campsite proprietor and not having the luxury of the internet in those days – oh how far off they seem - we took a chance most of the time. My lack of optimism was a bit of a drawback in this sort of trip, but my Other Half has bags of it and we always found somewhere safe to set up for the night. How he put up with my irrational fear of being set adrift in the middle of nowhere is a mystery to me.

We'd crossed the Spanish border near *Perpignan*, and after visiting the whimsical and I suppose *surreal Dalí* Museum at nearby *Figueres*, with a flourish I produced the *Mapa* and scoured its surface for campsite symbols.

"There's a site shown at *Banyoles*, a bit down the motorway towards *Barcelona*."

"That sounds as far as we want to go today. We'll go for it," Harry had done enough driving that day already.

I checked our large-scale motoring atlas for confirmation on which junction to get off at, and sat back to enjoy the scenery, at that point still congratulating myself for having the foresight to send away for the *Mapa*.

We took a rest-stop at the motorway services and discovered a large map of the area displayed there. This confirmed, yet again, that *Banyoles* had a campsite, but upon arrival in the town, there was no sign of a sign to one. People pottering in their gardens or walking dogs did not have a clue of the whereabouts of anything resembling a campsite in their neck of the woods when asked. This was disappointing, but all was not lost as I saw approaching us on the horizon, that group of *paseo-ing* ladies.

"One of them is bound to know!"

"I think you might be making a mistake!"

I jumped out of the van ignoring Harry's warnings.

He was right of course. As they all began arguing loudly amongst themselves about where one might be, they seemed to forget me. I crept away none the wiser, except to know not to ask a group of people directions again.

Deciding to cut our losses, we gave up on *Banyoles* and headed back to the motorway, direction *Barcelona*. With exquisitely bad timing, we found ourselves trying to negotiate our way from east to west of the *Catalan* capital just as all its citizens headed home in the Friday evening rush hour. Swept up in this manic display of driving meant that we missed exits for the coast where there would have presumably been a plethora of sites and we were in danger of bypassing Barcelona altogether. While we involuntarily hurtled along with the flow, I consulted the map again.

"There's a site shown near the airport."

"Well at least there are plenty of signs for that so we'll try to take the next one."

This did not guarantee that we were close to ending our journey for the day. The "next one" took us into the suburbs. Plenty of people to ask, but unfortunately none of them had a clue that there was a site remotely anywhere near. Well, they lived there after all, and had no need for one.

As it grew dark, rest that night looked like something as difficult to achieve as a Buddhist's *Nirvana*, but through a process of elimination eventually we struck lucky and on the central verge of a roundabout I caught sight of a tiny sign to the cheerfully named, *Camping Cala GoGo!* Any mild euphoria we were feeling soon melted as quickly as snow in summer though, because we found ourselves driving for some distance without further sight of directions to this fun-sounding place. We became quite a feature of this roundabout as we returned again and again taking the various options radiating from it.

Desperation by then made me even more illogical than usual, for with no better reason than that of family resemblance, I became convinced that a young man walking past, who reminded me of my brother, would be able to help. For once it seemed that in this case my unfounded hunch paid off. He confidently sent us back along one of the many roads already tried and given up on and it seemed that we'd previously thrown in the towel far too soon. This stretch of road did eventually run next to the perimeter fence of the airport and at length to the campsite. Even so we had to be reassured by the sight of a group of backpacking Aussies heading in the same direction that we weren't on a hiding to nothing.

Eventually we arrived at the *Cala GoGo*, but the presence of an armed security guard at the entrance was somewhat worrying. This was something unknown on any of the French places we'd stayed so far. We were past caring by then, and it would have made no difference to us if the place was run by the unexpected Spanish Inquisition. We'd arrived, the place looked decent which was all that mattered, and to top it all we had uniformed protection! Finding our pitch, in the dark the parallel lines of trees reminded me of *Ucello's* painting, *The Night Hunt*, though luckily hunting wasn't on the agenda. After rustling up a meal, we collapsed through the effects of that day's campsite quest, not to mention the bottle of wine and before that the large Cognacs we'd poured ourselves on arrival. The rest of the site took this as its cue to spring to life. Midnight approached, and the place still buzzed with music and the happy sounds of children playing. How Spanish!

If our campsite quest was traumatic enough around the most popular areas, at least there were people about to ask even though they were not always as reliable as we'd hoped. When our chosen way crossed the vast and mostly 'empty' centre of the peninsular it was another game altogether. And not one for the faint-hearted. Once a sign for 'camping' was spotted, the chances were that we would still be misled in some way or other. Distances mooted on such signs were invariably optimistically short compared to the reality of the situation. Even an enterprising crow flying there would have further to go than the number of metres/kilometres advertised. So it's no wonder that during our time in Spain, having negotiated unlikely looking tracks uphill and down I was almost always on the point of despair before we came across somewhere to stop, although by then it was not the site we had been aiming for in the first place.

On one occasion this confident shrinking of distances was reversed. We were driving through the middle of no-where when we noticed a freshly painted sign at the roadside with directions to a site that was "45, km" away. Thinking it was against the odds that they would bother to put up a sign for somewhere so far away, we decided it must have been a mistake. It was. In reality it was more like point 45 km away and we were almost on top of it. We got the feeling that the sign-writer may well have misplaced the 'dot' whilst over-indulging on his lunchtime *vinho*. Our lack of confidence in the veracity of the sign was rewarded by discovering one of the most picturesque places in Spain. This was *Alcalar de Júcar*. Set on the slopes of a deep ravine, which was the reason we'd failed to notice it up ahead, this dazzlingly white town was an amazing place to suddenly come across – we were in it before we saw it. The intriguingly deep emerald green *Júcar* river wound its way through the base of the valley, with steep and narrow streets climbing up the hillside and containing various tiny artisan shops such as bakers and potters. Even the campsite was nigh on perfect. Being next to the river, the cool atmosphere created by rushing water was not a problem at first, but a little worrying later when a storm got up. Torrential rain turned the gently flowing *Júcar* into something frighteningly more suitable for white-water rafting. Was this place on our *Mapa*? We never did find out.

This type of happy, by chance discovery, otherwise known I suppose as 'serendipity', happened on several occasions. At *Córdoba* for instance, a campsite sign led us onto a newly built estate of rather nice detached villas, but the fact that the road ended in a pile of aggregate made us suspect that the site was too valuable for such cheap activities as camping, and been swallowed up by the monster of suburban expansion. On our return to the main road, we spotted another signpost laying down on the central verge which appeared to have been floored by a careless motorist or a local with a grudge, but unsure as to which way round it was meant to stand before this act of vandalism, we were no closer to our overnight stop.

Leaving *Córdoba* behind us, we travelled for some distance up the narrow road of a small mountain with sinking hearts. Our reward this time was a lovely pine-wooded site set on the top of it. I don't think that this was the place which the fallen sign post was indicating since it was well outside the limits of the town, but who cared? The usual mad weekend influx of local campers on a Friday night was anticipated, but as only a few couples and small families turned up, peace reigned completely during that pine-scented evening. *Villares* was one of the most peaceful and pleasantly simple sites which we came across in Spain, further enhanced by the proprietor re-opening the bar specially for me to use the phone when he saw us walking away from the public one which *no funcionár*. I think it may have helped however, when I mentioned that it was my *'Madre'* that I was attempting to ring. In Spain, mothers really are held in high esteem.

By the time we crossed the border and arrived back in France almost three weeks later, it was no wonder we cracked open a bottle of Champagne. Our enthusiasm to repeat the adventure in the near future was lukewarm to say the least. But like childbirth, the pain and inconvenience was soon forgotten, and not being able to find a buyer for the van, we felt that Italy should be our destination for the following year.

Italy was campsite paradise. Well, there were loads of them anyway. The Italians take camping, especially in camper-vans, as seriously as they do football and Opera, so the struggle to find stopping places was no-where near as frustrating as it had been in Spain. We loved Italy. *There they had learnt the dark art of putting a signpost where it actually can be seen.*

Space-tales from Under the Awning

Ever wondered where the idea of a *Tardis* may have come from? Can you fit three 20-stone adults in a Fiat 500? These questions and many other things we didn't particularly want to know the answers to either, were solved during our time on various sites around Southern Europe.

Tardis?

Late one afternoon on the *Torre Pendente* site in *Pisa*, we were pouring ourselves another glass of well-chilled *Soave* in an attempt to decide our menu for the evening meal. This laborious task was disturbed by the arrival opposite of a German registered Volvo Estate: the perfect vehicle for transporting camping equipment in, so nothing remarkable about that. A family of six spilled out, but that was just the prologue. Raising glasses to our mouths, we paused mid-lift at the scene unfolding before us.

Piles of camping paraphernalia appeared on the pitch's dusty sward. We'd no idea where all that stuff had come from, but with no other vehicle in sight, the Volvo was our prime suspect.

We looked at each other, amazed. How had this normal-looking estate contained the following? :
- two adults
- four children
- tables

- chairs
- tents
- ground sheets
- sleeping bags
- stoves
- cool boxes

I'm certain there were bikes as well, but surely this must have been straying into the realms of fantasy?

The usual scene when families arrived at a campsite was for Mum and Dad to do all the work – the children running round excitedly getting in the way and only really interested in unpacking anything to find the tennis racquets. But our Volvo family were different. They were the *Von Trapp* family before Julie Andrews got her hands on them. Father even resembled Christopher Plummer. Within a gnat's crotchet, order was made from all that stuff which had so mysteriously materialised from no-where. Each child, no matter how young, knew exactly what to do without being told. Not one of them whinged that so-and-so was slacking, and no child sat playing on its *Gameboy* whilst everyone else did all the work.

"Don't stare," Harry suggested, though I noticed he couldn't resist glancing in their direction.

It was compelling though. They were automatons. So this was how the famous German work-ethic operates, a bit like the Jesuits: get 'em young.

"I'll bet they worked it all out on their drive before they left home," my Other Half obviously was taking more interest in them than he'd been letting on. "He'd have measured everything and decided on the best fit!"

"Well I can just imagine him with a whistle and clip-board commanding those poor kids like something from *The Sound of Music*. Liesl – tent pegs! Kurt – groundsheets!"

Hunger soon meant that our attention was taken up with knocking up some pasta and salad, but it wasn't too long before we sat down under the awning outside to eat. The *Von Trapps* had by then prepared, eaten and cleared away their meal, and were heading off into Pisa (on bikes?) presumably for some sight-seeing. How we admired their energy.

Our evening was taken up by sharing a drink or two with a young English couple on their gap-year, and by the time we turned in for the night there was no sign of our well-organised neighbours. Next morning, bright but not too early, I peeped out of the van's front window. I blinked in disbelief. The pitch opposite was vacant. I looked to right and left. Nothing.

"You're not going to believe this," I said.

"Try me,"

"Take a look. The *Von Trapps* have gone!"

We pulled back the curtain. There was nothing left but an old chair I'd noticed the day before that had been commandeered to support the cooker. This family was so efficient. With the same quiet precision they used upon arrival, they had vacated the annexed pitch and the site.

"Maybe I shouldn't say this but … the Germans were always good at swift occupation!"

"But maybe not always so fast at leaving!"

It's like being in the front row at the RSC on a campsite. You just can't help yourself.

Three 20-stone adults in a *Fiat 500*?

Another Tardis-type illusion had presented itself the previous year in Spain.

The *Despeñaperros* national park, to the North of *Granada*, is spectacular. After a nerve-racking drive on a high altitude, winding mountain pass, we reached the site at the small town of *Santa Elena*. Each pitch on site was surrounded with pine-trees and as in many places, devoid of grass. Instead pinecones, needles and twigs studded the ground, not to mention rocks and stones, but such flooring didn't affect us as travellers in a campervan. It would be a little uncomfortable though for those in tents.

With the sun cresting the mountain peaks, we were lounging under the awning recovering from that particularly breath-taking drive and an especially good meal, gazing disinterestedly across the site. A small and elderly *Fiat* 500 trundled onto a pitch in our sight-line and two large and elderly occupants climbed out. A slightly younger man, also super-sized, extricated himself from the back seat. Not especially interesting you might be thinking, but they held our attention as the three of them began to scour the floor of their chosen pitch, enlisting the help of some sort of groundsman who was passing by. All of them seemed quite happy in their task, and their laughter echoed round the site.

"Do you think they've lost something?" I asked.

"They'll have a job finding anything small on this ground."

If they hadn't been enjoying themselves so much, the scene might have resembled one of those 'fingertip' searches you see on the news, where overall clad police officers crawl around a field on their hands and knees.

After some time, our jolly *CSI* team seemed to give up the task, the groundsman drove off on his dinky-toy tractor and the *Fiat* three opened the car boot. Minute in itself, from its shallow depths they unloaded a small igloo-type tent like magicians producing a rabbit from a hat. In an instant this was erected.

"Surely they're not going to sleep in that?" I mused, "There's no way all three could sit in it let alone lay down! Maybe one of them's going to sleep in the car, but look how small that is!"

"Well maybe you should go and ask them as you're so interested!"

Talk about the pot calling the kettle black.

With nothing else to speculate about, as the family sat down to prepare their meal over a diminutive camping stove, we lost interest. It was soon rekindled though when we realised the woman was taking a turn around the site, visiting each pitch. I couldn't wait for her to approach us, as I was curious to know what her mission was. With her gypsy looks, lucky heather and fortune-telling would have been my guess, but I was wrong.

She waved a plastic carrier bag at us. The Andalucian roll of the tongue is so fascinating to listen to. Soft yet at the same time harsh and rapid.

"*Porrrrfavorrrr - Harrrrrrrrrrrrrarrrrrra?*"

We sat smiling in admiration. We couldn't understand a word. There followed an embarrassingly suggestive mime, succeeded by the *pièce de résistance* - a blow-up bed produced from the bag. The penny eventually dropped. A hand pump. Unfortunately, we had no such thing on board.

"*Lo siento, no hay.*" I shook my head.

These being some of the few Spanish words I knew, I was pleased in one way to be using them, but in another way I wasn't. Being taken up by their goings-on opposite, I'd become fond of the trio. They seemed so happy to be on the site with their tiny faded tent and little primus stove. I felt heroic cooking with two rings, an oven and a grill, and the accommodation in our van was positively palatial compared to their living arrangements. Sitting on our fold-up chairs gave me back-ache, but they were content to sit on the stony ground.

The mystery of their sleeping arrangements remained so, because once the profound mountain darkness fell, it was impossible to see much further than our own windows. I hoped they located that pump. Assuming that they didn't manage to clear all the stones and pine needles from their pitch, someone could have had a lumpy bed that night.

For obvious reasons most of life *on the road* is carried on in 'the open'. The vantage point from the inside of a caravan or underneath the relative protection of the awning, provides a discreet window on the surrounding microcosm. You might not wish to be a voyeur, but often you have no choice. Of course, the reverse is also true. The worst time for this is upon arrival at a site. Those already established and sitting outside on their little fold-up chairs (complete with fire buckets at the ready if they are Brits) showed great interest in our frustrating search to find an electricity connection which actually worked. You could almost hear them saying to each other,

"Let's see how many times they have to move before they give up!"

It was embarrassing driving from pitch to pitch in search of this essential item, but with experience comes wisdom. Rather than making a show of ourselves, Harry soon learnt to prowl the vacant pitches with the *multi-meter of truth* in hand, on a heroic quest to find that elusive "viable 220 volt readout". With just him becoming the object of interest rather than myself, this suited me no end.

Shakespeare once wrote: "All the World's a Stage…" I would add, "*…especially on a campsite.*"

Et in Arcadia Ego

There is a fascinating painting by the 17th century artist, Poussin. In it, four beautiful patrician-looking shepherds, draped in elegant, classical garb, are depicted discovering a tomb surrounded by the idyllic Italianate *campagne*. Some raise their hands, and all look at each other in a gesture of query, seemingly at a loss to know the purpose of this alien object. The Latin inscription on the tomb and the title of the work, *"Et in Arcadia ego"*, can be translated as:

"*I* (therefore Death), *am also in Arcadia"*

Arcadia then, deemed to be the place of earthly paradise, turns out to have a down side after all. There were a few '*Et in Arcadia*' moments in store for us during our travels.

For the most part, it was vaguely amusing incidents which enlivened our hours at leisure in the relative protection of a campsite. There were times though when unsavoury occurrences infiltrated even these havens, serving as a reminder that this was the real world after all and not some *Disney* inspired travelogue. Added to this, the sight of numerous short-skirted, high-heeled, dusky-skinned girls loitering on remote lay-bys throughout Italy also brought me down to earth. At first I could be heard innocently thinking out loud,

"She's got a long wait for a bus out here!"

It didn't take long for me to put two and two together and realise that it wasn't exactly that kind of ride she was waiting for. If, before we left home I had been under the romantic impression that Italy was some sort of Renaissance theme park, then this was my wake-up call.

A campsite south of the Italian town of *Como*, a place set on a lovely Alpine lake, unfortunately also became the setting of a particularly nasty *"Et in Arcadia"* moment. This site was fairly small, but quite attractive with grassy areas, large leafy trees for shade and a good sized swimming pool. That day being hot, the pool was naturally a magnet for the children staying there. I myself was looking forward to a swim once we'd sorted ourselves out, but first I decided it was necessary to find some fresh drinking water. I prowled the grounds in search of a standpipe, holding my plastic bottle before me like a *Hare Krishna* begging bowl, until I realised I was wasting my time. I must have looked a fool searching for something which those already there knew didn't exist. The usual scattering of standpipes normally planted around these places for the convenience of inmates was conspicuous by its absence. My only option now was to seek out the washing-up shed as the only water-based option left, but the nauseating smell in there when I found it, left me wondering if I'd accidentally wandered into the lavatories. Did they really expect people to wash their plates there? But if the dish place had been disgusting, something even more unsavoury was to come.

I began to make my way back to the van in the forlorn hope that I would discover a fresh water source elsewhere, when a car zoomed into the site. Reminiscent of a scene from *Starsky and Hutch*, it screeched to a halt in a cloud of dust next to where I was walking. Two men jumped out, but they were nothing like those two handsome American detectives. It would seem unfair to judge people by their outward appearance, but the occupants of this car might have looked more at home rising up from a grave in the *'Thriller'* video. Charles Dickens himself would have been proud to invent this pair of grotesques - they *literally* gave me the creeps. I quickened my pace wanting to get as far away as possible, so at first I didn't realise they were trying to attract my attention.

"*Scusi. Scusi, signora!*"

Instead of using my common sense by ignoring them, I turned round. They seemed to be asking me something, but spoke so rapidly that I couldn't understand a word of it. I shrugged my shoulders,

"*Scusi, non capisco,*" I said, doubting that I'd got the expression correct in my attempt to make a quick getaway. I certainly didn't want to get involved in any discussion with *Squeers* and *Quilp*. Becoming exasperated, they called after me again, but this time I shrugged, pointed to the reception hut and fled. They certainly looked like a couple of weirdos, but I thought no more about them – until later.

From our pitch, we had a reasonable view of the swimming pool, and shortly after my water-less return, I was surprised to see these two gentlemen, drinks in hand, entering the pool enclosure. With the swagger of *San Tropez* playboys they sat themselves down, the younger of them now in swimming trunks. Intrigued by the gruesome twosome, I noticed they were taking more than a casual interest in the children having fun in and out of the water and began to have serious doubts about their motive for being poolside. I pointed them out to Harry.

"Those weird fellas by the pool. Don't you think they look a bit suspicious?" I asked, and proceeded to tell him about my earlier encounter.

"Well they do look a bit odd, but live and let live and all that,"

"Just look at the way they keep staring at those kids," I said, "and that one seems to be getting them to climb out of the pool and chat to him."

Something about all this was just not right.

"I know you think it's just my imagination, but they seemed a nasty pair."

For once I was not the only one with a suspicious mind that hot afternoon. It wasn't long before we were roused from our lethargy by shouting: the dynamic duo were being confronted by a group of adults apparently in charge of some of the children. The situation soon began to turn even uglier than two of the protagonists. Some of the men in the group were trying to persuade the pair to leave in a more hands on manner. It was getting more fraught than a Christmas episode of *EastEnders* when the local *polizia* made their appearance centre stage. Having the authority to be more 'persuasive' than the civilians, they grabbed *Squeers* and *Quilp* by the arms and dragged them out of the pool area. The drama concluded for us with the pair being manhandled into the waiting police car and driven away.

"Well, you were right for once in your life," said my Other Half, giving me a supportive hug.

I just wished I'd been wrong this time though. These really were the local 'perverts'. We were left wondering if this was a regular occurrence as there didn't seem to be any discussion taking place before they were bundled away so unceremoniously. Maybe the police couldn't be bothered to charge them, just 'picked them up' occasionally and carted them off as the need arose.

This incident was disturbing enough, though as the day wore on it began to pale into insignificance. Something else we felt more menacing to everyone there took its place high in the anxiety stakes.

Throughout the late afternoon and into the evening we gradually became aware that a non-stop stream of caravans and campers had been arriving. At first, this was unremarkable as sites often filled up as night time approached and travellers decided to finish their journey for the day. When we'd arrived there soon after midday, we had carte blanche when it came to deciding where to set up, choosing a pleasantly shaded spot at the edge of the place. Although the space we occupied was not exactly large, even including the area under our awning, with this constant influx of vehicles we began to feel like landed gentry. Newcomers were now being crammed into spaces that did not before appear to be spaces at all. All this it seemed was with the consent of the proprietors, because we saw them directing people in campervans to park on the roadway through lack of anywhere else for them to stop. Whether their motivation to allow this hazardous practice was through a genuine wish to accommodate travellers or to cash in on the huge numbers of mostly Dutch nationals descending on the site we couldn't tell - though we were cynical enough to think the latter. If we hadn't already put up our awning and boldly placed our table and chairs under it, we were certain that someone would have put a tent there while we were absent making phone calls later. I certainly wouldn't have relished doing a *Sherpa Tensing* impression up the side of it to get into our van.

The place began to resemble a refugee camp in a Third World country. Clouds of smoke rose from stoves and barbeques, with families cooking, eating and drinking in the narrow spaces in front and between them. Harry began to see the worrying side to all this.

"God help us if a fire starts here."

Previously, the absence of water around the site was merely an inconvenience. Now it was something serious. With all those fires and stoves so near the tents, surely it wasn't just us who thought it was more than a bit dangerous for those packs of children to act like they were in an adventure playground. Even though we usually poked fun at the over-the-top way British Camping/Caravanning clubs are cautious of over-crowding, this seemed preferable at that moment.

"The Caravan Club would have a heart attack if they saw this place!"

Tennis and football tournaments were now being inaugurated in the roadways, but the sight of balls flying around so close to fire seemed unremarkable to the *Beckers, Beckhams* and their supporters.

"The worst thing is, there aren't even any standpipes. It's a disaster waiting to happen!"

Nothing else appeared to have been provided on site for putting out fires, such as buckets of sand, and now I was getting really worried. British caravanners (not us) loved to sit outside their units with a handy little-red-bucket proudly displayed.

"Those little buckets would be no good in this situation. I doubt even if a hose would do anything in this place now."

"Well the *'twenty-foot-between-each-unit'* enthusiasts would be having apoplexy!"

This was usually the same lot as the fire bucket brigade. To be within elbowing distance from their neighbours would be their nightmare. It was turning into ours.

I could see Harry deep in thought. The worried look on his face made me realise that the situation really was nothing to joke about.

"What can we do, apart from leave?"

He'd realised that the whole site was completely enclosed by a very high and dense hedge behind an equally high chain link fence. The only things that could use this as a thoroughfare were the birds.

"Well the only thing to do would be for me to drive the van up as close to the hedge as I can and we could climb onto the roof and …"

I stopped him there.

"I'm not designed to climb up or over anything higher than a stile!" I moaned.

"I think you could if the worse came to the worst," he said.

He had a point.

Were we the only people that night feeling uneasy about the situation, or was it just an in-built British caution making the danger seem obvious? We were left wondering if camping and caravanning organisations in other countries had the same high regard for the *'20 foot rule'* as ours did. No one else appeared to be bothered enough to let it spoil their night.

Things of course did not seem so bad in the clear light of the next morning, but all the same, we never wanted to experience being trapped in such a potentially dangerous situation again. Despite the fire-hazards, the perverts and the smelly facilities, we liked the place, but if the alternative another time was stay there or travel on through the night, I know which course we would have chosen.

Et in Aranjuez ego

Italian campsites did not have a monopoly on less-than-savoury goings-on. The previous year, we discovered a seedy side to the pleasant site bordering the river *Tajo* at *Aranjuez* in Spain. But if gravity applied to the darker side at *Como,* levity could certainly describe the goings-on at *Aranjuez.*

Aranjuez was a welcoming place. Its parks and verges were reminiscent of their English counterparts with tall leafy trees, swathes of grass and well stocked flower beds.

"This place looks like home!" I gushed excitedly as we drove into the town. Everywhere was so green and pleasant.

"They've even got a Dotto train!"

Unfortunately, we'd left our recording of *Rodrigo's* guitar *concierto* in the rack at home, but it was too tempting not to sing the opening bars of the haunting slow movement – *la la laar, la la la laa la la la, la la laar.*

The place was buzzing with a holiday atmosphere which we realised was due to European elections taking place the following day. Why we don't celebrate our own elections with carousels and bunting I'll never know, but then Democracy in Spain was still a novelty then. The large open parade ground at the centre of town, where the candidates had been holding their rallies, was the starting point for that 'Dotto' train. In a similar way to the one in our own seaside towns, though about as far from the sea as you can get in Spain, it was packed with balloon wielding children, adding to the festive atmosphere. Such cheerfulness must have been catching for we too found ourselves for once in a happy frame of mind, a rare occurrence at that late stage in our Spanish sojourn.

Particularly impressive was that directions to the campsite had been thoughtfully posted on the door of the tourist office, which needless to say was itself closed for the duration. As was the local *Castillo* and an exhibition of works by Spain's, and arguably the Western World's, most important artist, *Velasquez*. How disappointing. Not for the first time had we arrived somewhere when something interesting was closed, or before it had opened, missing these things by hours. Once, we managed to be too late and too early at the same time. This was in *Le Câteau*, the birthplace of *Matisse* in Northern France. There they'd just begun to dismantle the *Matisse* Museum and had yet to start on the new one. *C'est la vie, n'est pas?*

Back in *Aranjuez*, the site, like the town, boasted some splendid trees, and was pleasantly unregimented in that we could just stop where we wanted. At first we put down our roots next to a lovely tall and ancient oak near the river, but the sight of storm clouds and the sound of distant thunder, plus the usual swarms of gnats next to water (not to mention the large clan of chain-smokers parked nearby) was enough to make us pack everything up again and seek out yet another part of the site. Away from the river there was an area with 'permanent' tented dwellings but with plenty of vacant grassy spaces between, it was no hardship to take up a place next to an unoccupied one of these. We seemed to have found the ideal place to stop for a few days.

That Saturday night also coincided with a wedding party at a restaurant in the park on the opposite side of the river. We'd seen the happy couple being photographed earlier in these picturesque surroundings, shadowed by a lady of a certain age, presumably the mother-of-the-bride. In her full Spanish flamenco regalia, her scowl was as black as her Mantilla headdress.

"Poor bloke," Harry murmured after we'd passed the trio. "He looks like a nice guy. Fancy having her as a mother-in-law!"

Loud and extremely cheesy music with its accompanying revelries serenaded us well into the night thanks to these possibly ill-advised nuptials. It was always annoying to hear people having a good time and not be able to join in. Still, we felt sure that Sunday would be peaceful, and for once we'd not been troubled by bells, clocks or barking dogs. What we hadn't foreseen was that the army barracks down the road would choose Sunday night to hold its machine gun practice. But hey, you can't have everything.

That following Monday still being a holiday, the site soon filled with happy picnicking families. Unfortunately their day out was curtailed abruptly when the heavens opened with the rain-storm that had been threatening since our arrival in *Aranjuez*. While they hurriedly packed away their hampers and other picnic paraphernalia, they watched in amazement as we perversely danced about in the rain. For us this was manna from heaven, not being big fans of the unmitigated heat and wall to wall sunshine of Southern Spain. After almost three weeks all we wanted was a good old English downpour. Our excitement was short-lived though, because disappointingly the torrent stopped as abruptly as it had started.

It was then that we noticed a car had drawn up outside the 'permanent' next to us. Although there was nothing unusual about this, the undue haste with which the couple jumped out of the car and disappeared into the tent with heads down and glancing neither left nor right like celebs trying to avoid the *paparazzi* made them appear a little suspicious. Since the skies were by now completely clear, they were not trying to keep dry. No bags or any of the usual stuff accompanying 'campers' were in evidence, once inside they didn't raise any of the curtains at the tent 'windows', and the entrance flaps remained firmly shut. To all intents (sorry!) and purposes the place was still unoccupied.

Harry being more cynical than even I am, was convinced our fellow 'holiday-makers' weren't there for the good of their health.

"You'll see", he said, "they'll only be here a couple of hours. We've chosen to stop next to the local *knocking shop!*"

I didn't want to believe this but a short while later as I sat outside reading and enjoying the rain-refreshed early evening air, the man emerged from his lair. The sudden movement made me look up, and I unfortunately caught his sheepish glance in my direction. As is usual in such a situation, I politely made the effort to say "good evening", but my *"Buenos"* was obviously unwelcome. All I got in return was an indecipherable grunt as he made a bee-line for the toilet block. A few minutes later he was followed in the same direction by a peroxided blonde of indeterminable age, tastefully dressed in a tight leopard skin top and short leather skirt, face wearing 'full slap'. Her legs were as wobbly as the newly born *Bambi* as she awkwardly tottered across the rough grass on her stiletto heels. Within minutes of them both arriving back from the 'facilities', they'd jumped into the car again and driven away.

"See I told you!"

Somehow I get the feeling that I'm too naïve.

"...we got a problem..." Part One
Small Problems

So there we were, stranded with our van in the middle of a vast and near deserted 'Park & Ride' in *Pisa*, the tarmac radiating enough heat to cook a four course meal with. I was panicking as usual but Harry sat there in the driver's seat looking like a particularly cool Clint Eastwood as he weighed up the options.

"Well, can you fix it?" I asked hopefully.

Then I spotted a mirage. Well it wasn't actually a mirage - more a fortuitous co-incidence – but anyway it was rather miraculous.

An excellent way to extend your vocabulary in a foreign language beyond the usual alcohol-buying or direction-enquiring phrases, is to have a mechanical breakdown. Travelling in our camper van would not have been the same without the odd 'technical hitch' to enrich the experience.

"Think of it as a good way to get to talk to different people and practise your language skills," was the spin my Other Half put on it.

He would have done well in the government press office. But even though Harry could usually be relied on to sort things out, occasionally the problem required something beyond even his inventive powers.

When it comes to anything technical I haven't a clue. Despite all Harry's efforts to educate me over the years, all I really know about cars is how to drive one. If truth be told, only my own car really, so when it fell to me to explain a mechanical problem in a foreign language, this complete ignorance of how anything works was a big disadvantage. It would have been difficult enough in English.

Throughout Spain in our first year of travel in the *Leyland Daf*, the 'leisure' battery had been a giving us trouble[1]. We'd been assured by the previous owner that this was a new battery. Like most things he assured us about though, the truth was being stretched rather thinly. Everything was new once. Basically, the van's electronics were rubbish. While we had been enjoying ourselves in the *Campo dei Miracoli* trying to get that shot of the Leaning Tower balancing drunkenly on our hands, the whole lot expired. The main battery feeding the starter, lights etc., was completely dead. The leisure battery was comatose. Nothing had been charging at all during that week's lengthy journey to get to Pisa. Brilliant.

Now comes the 'mirage'. It was almost as miraculous as the *Campo* we'd just returned from. Across the car park we could see that one of the buses which was the 'ride' part of our 'Park and Ride', seemed to be having mechanical problems and the local bus depot had sent out its Man and Van.

"I'm sure they'd give us a jump start!" I exclaimed, almost delirious with new found confidence. I knew that much about vehicles anyway, and was determined not to let this bit of luck pass us by. What came over me at that moment I'll never know. Taking on a completely new persona I grabbed the jump-leads that Harry had just retrieved from the *Calor-gas* locker and dashed towards the broken down bus. Its defective engine by then had become a magnet for a dozen or more other drivers and hangers-on.

At times like this, any knowledge of a language I have decides to take its own holiday. Being confronted by a sea of faces simultaneously turning to see this desperate-looking female waving a pair of jump leads at them, had my smattering of Italian packing its bags and heading for the airport.

"*Per Favore!*" was all I could think of.

Luckily this was all that was necessary. The mechanic took one look at me and had pity. He drove the breakdown van over to us leaving the dead bus to its own devices, and like over-grown children following the Pied Piper, the rest of the broken-down-bus club swiftly followed. They seemed pleased to have a new bonnet to look under, and soon the crowd of petrol-heads around our van began to resemble a *Top Gear* audience. Our new friend attached the leads to the right bits of two huge batteries in the back of his van, but to everyone's amazement, these proved to be about as good as ours. **No** good that is.

"Just our luck", I whinged, now back in my normal frame of mind.

Still in Clint mode, Harry then suggested trying the more modestly sized battery in the breakdown van's own engine. When this did the trick, anyone seeing my relief would think we'd been stranded in the wild's of Borneo for a month rather than the half an hour in a car park.

"*Mille Grazie!*" I gushed, far too many times. I wanted to make sure he knew just how grateful I was. It was at this point that Harry felt the need to explain to the man why our battery was flat.

"Tell him in Italian that *blah blah* is not doing *such and such*,"

If Harry didn't mind getting me into confusing conversations, I did. It always put me in mind of *Basil Fawlty* saying, "*My wife will explain*". Since our saviour did not speak a great deal of English, I had no choice but to try though. He nodded and "*Si, Si*"d in all the salient places, but of course, customary holiday vocabulary was not up to the job of a technical conversation. Many avenues of misunderstanding were explored with my Other Half pointing to certain parts of the engine like an Open University lecturer to illustrate each point he was telling me to translate. I began to feel that I would spend *the rest of my life* having that conversation and called a halt. We were ready to be back on the road again and whether that nice chap understood why our van hadn't started mattered not in the slightest to me. Or to him probably.

Problems other than those to do with engines also dogged those early trips. Appropriately at the spa town of *Montecatini Termi*, we had a wet awakening one morning. The water pump for the sink sprung a leak while we slumbered, with the result that Harry had an unexpected paddle when he got up to make the tea. As usual, there was an upside to this small hitch. This time it was the caravan supplies business we found in town; an Aladdin's cave of everything one could need, plus many things one didn't know one needed for life on the road. The Italians have a particular penchant for camper vans, and seeing the incredible gin palaces on wheels offered for sale at this emporium made us feel somewhat dissatisfied with our own set-up.

"I expect you'd like one of those," Harry knew me only too well.

"Well you could put a small car into those rear lockers! That would solve the problem of getting around all those narrow lanes we've had to avoid."

It seemed a bit of a set-back when we lost our reverse gear, and all but one of the forward ones, in the middle of *Chartres* one year. Only a few days into our trip, we'd pulled onto one of those wide, tree-lined, parking verges that grace the boulevards of French cities to consult the map. When we tried to back onto the road, the van decided that it would much prefer to go forwards. Fortunately it being a Sunday, there was not much traffic about on those usually busy thoroughfares. Harry realised there was no way he could get it into gear by using the gear stick, and had to crawl underneath the vehicle, where he manually rammed it into reverse. Now he could reverse it across the road onto the opposite verge so that at least we were pointing in the right direction. Then in the same manner as before, he rammed it into the remaining forward gear.

At a snail's pace we tentatively set off to find the local Municipal campsite using only second gear, praying that we wouldn't need reverse again before we got there. This was not as easy a task as it sounds because apart from the difficulty of pulling away from the many sets of traffic lights in the city using the wrong gear, our planned route was continually scuppered by no entry signs and one way streets which were not shown as such on those street plans thoughtfully dotted around the city.

We eventually limped onto the site and established ourselves for what we thought might be an extended stay. Luckily it was ideally situated - close to the river and with a footpath making an easy walk to the Cathedral and that other essential destination, the supermarket. With the weather deciding to improve itself at last, we began to feel that we could not have been stranded in a better place. Harry knew he could fix things easily once he had the right spare-part, so having rung *Europ Assistance* and described exactly what was needed, I felt relaxed about the situation. Even though we'd experienced plenty of mechanical problems in the past, this was the first time we actually needed to enlist the help of our insurance company to get us out of a 'fix'.

Later that day though, the sleepy site was roused by the appearance of a large breakdown truck. *Europ Assistance* had got their wires crossed and enlisted the services of the local man and breakdown truck to take the van away. Once more I was obliged to engage in the usual complicated discussion about car mechanics in a foreign language. The driver's young son sat excitedly in the cab, enjoying the experience of accompanying his Dad on a 'job'. Luckily he was more interested in messing about with the controls inside the cab than watching me struggle to explain why we didn't need his Dad's help. If we'd wanted to get our money's worth out of the insurance premium, we could have installed ourselves in a nice hotel and sent the company the bill. But we were quite happy to do what we would have been doing anyway, with or without gears. *Chartres* has a beautiful cathedral, and it was no hardship to have plenty of time to explore the City and relax afterwards with a bottle of wine and a pleasant river-side meal. As yet, we were in no rush to get to our intended destination of Florence.

Having disturbed his Sunday, the truck driver seemed disappointed to leave without our van *en panne*, but it was not our fault that *Europ Assistance* had wanted to overdo the *assistance* bit. We kept our fingers crossed that the correct part would arrive, but obviously nothing could happen until the next day. We spent that Monday doing the tourist thing, and over all having a very pleasant time.

The correct part was sent out from England by plane on the Monday and delivered to us by late Tuesday lunchtime. Impressive. But by then the weather had again taken a turn for the worse. There can be few things more depressing than sitting cooped up inside a tin box with the rain drumming on it like some kind of Chinese torture. My family had done this enough times in English seaside caravans when I was little and I was not keen to relive that particular piece of childhood nostalgia.

A mere half an hour later, my hero had fixed the new part, we had all our gears, and were ready for the off.

"Can you dig out that Sixties compilation I made?" he said.

I dug it out of the dashboard clutter.

"No prizes for guessing which track you want to play!" I said as I put it in the player.

"Well I'm sorry 'bout you cryin' but I'm off
On the Road Again! (On the Road Again)..."

And so we were.

That particular bit on the tape was in danger of becoming worn out.

One of my favourite bits of our van's equipment almost came to its untimely end while we were staying the following year at *Niederbrun,* north of *Strasbourg*. It was a dramatic conclusion to our evening. The rumbling of distant thunder accompanied our *al fresco* meal on that quiet, wooded site. We both loved storms. When I was very young, rather than cowering under a table like frightened rabbits, my sister and I were always encouraged to stand at the front door watching the lightening. For some reason, a child safety gate put across the opening gave us a sense of security, and because of this, I'm grateful there's at least one thing in life that some people are frightened of and I am not.

At *Niederbrun,* the sight of lightening flashing between distant black clouds was promising, and with the night being warm we thought it would be a good idea to remain outside with the awning protecting us from the rain. We'd done this during a storm at *Punta Sabbioni* on the *Venice* lagoon the previous year whilst everyone else on the site had disappeared into their various tents and caravans etc. We were made of sterner stuff and hammered down the pegs, determined to sit it out while hell broke out in the skies above us.

This time it was different. Instead of that breezy Italian storm, the wind in the *Alsace* was steadily increasing in violence, and my comfort zone under the awning shrunk. The gusts were becoming really scary.

"Maybe we should call it a night and go in now," I said.

"Yes, you're right. This doesn't look too good does it?"

For once we were in agreement about something that worried me.

Fate however decided things for us. A sudden whirlwind lifted the awning and threw it up and over the van as easily as if it had been a discarded newspaper. Despite the rain reaching monsoon proportions, we had to try to rescue it and with the table and chairs now also in imminent danger of being carried off it was hard to know where to turn first. Harry somehow managed to retrieve the awning, which had been flapping about madly like a spinnaker in a hurricane while it was draped over the top of the van. I wrestled our table and chairs into submission and threw them underneath, hoping they wouldn't be carried off to add to the confusion. Harry shouted instructions at me, but I could barely hear him over the lashing rain and hurricane-force wind. He was wrestling himself now, but with one side of the pole that the awning rolled round for stowage.

"Grab the other end!"

"We can't do it!" I yelled, the wind throwing my words back at me. "I can't even stand up!"

"Yes we can!" he yelled back, sounding like a manic Bob the Builder.

By now I was in hysterics, not knowing whether to laugh or cry, but somehow I did manage to take hold of the other end and between us we rolled the thing up, though understandably not as neatly as in normal circumstances.

By the time we'd climbed back into the van and shut the door behind us, we were soaked to the skin and thoroughly exhausted from our battle with the elements and the awning. We looked at each other and then it wasn't just me who became hysterical.

"You look a right state. Like a drowned rat!" my gallant husband shouted between gasps, trying to make himself heard above the rain crashing down on the van roof.

"Well if I look like one, I wouldn't want to say what you look like," I screamed above the din, "I know how it feels to enter a Miss Wet Tee-shirt Contest now!" I'd never been so wet fully clothed before.

Once we'd dried ourselves off - not as easy as it sounds, staggering about with laughter in a confined space - we too were obliged to storm-watch from relative safety inside the van. In the glorious sunshine of the next morning, it seemed difficult to believe that there had been such a violent end to the previous day. Despite its adventure, our precious awning was undamaged, and we decided that maybe we should give it a little more consideration in future storm-watching.

The brightness of the day though belied the tragedy that had happened the night before just a few miles down the road in a Strasbourg park. We heard on the news that 10 people had been killed when a tree fell on a marquee during the height of the storm. With this in mind, we realised that the tree-filled site at *Niederbrun*, had not been the safest place to sit out a storm – especially in the open.

Notes
(1) For the uninformed, or in case anyone is actually interested, the 'Leisure' battery is a second battery which feeds the lights etc inside the van when on site so that the main battery does not become discharged and is always ready to start the vehicle.

"…we got a problem…" Part Two

It is the stuff of nightmares. Brakes failing on a mountain road. Smoke billowing from the wheels and exhaust pipe. No-where to go but down. But this was no bad dream, and it happened to us twice.

The drive up the slopes of Mount Vesuvius is long, winding and tedious, so having reached the end of the road, the sight of a car park there is more than a bit of a relief. At that moment, the unsuspecting tourist willingly parts with his cash in order to get to his objective, even though it does seem like a lot of money to fork out. From the car park, he must then take the dusty path onwards and upwards. He doesn't mind – he is on his way to see a volcano. They haven't finished with him yet though. Any further progress is halted by an entry booth – yes, to the volcano. On the same principle as that used for parking, the assumption must be that having already walked hundreds of yards uphill, our friend the tourist will not be deterred from reaching his goal, now so tantalisingly close he can smell the sulphur. How could he return home after visiting the bay of Naples and Pompeii without also having ascended to the crater of Vesuvius?

We had little cash to spare when we arrived half-way up the side of Vesuvius[1], and decided to leave our van on the approach road rather than the car park. Having to pay to reach the top came as an unpleasant surprise, but since we'd not been fleeced by the car park owners, like everyone else we too decided that having come so far, our only option was to grin and cough up. I brandished my credit card through the hut window.

"Sorry, no cards madame! We have no electricity up here." The man at the booth spoke impeccable English.

"We have no *Lire*," I explained. "Our cash was stolen in Rome."

Because this was a Sunday, we hadn't been able to find a bank open since leaving the capital city the day before. But all was not lost. Hearing our hard luck tale, he was sympathetic.

"I will take another currency if you wish."

How kind. I retrieved a ten pound note from the depths of my bag. Well, it was a small price to pay, and if the exchange rate wasn't great, we'd given up trying to get the best deal on everything about 200 miles ago.

We passed through the entrance arch where an avuncular elderly gentleman was handing out tall rustic walking sticks, laughing and cheerily patting people on the back as he did so.

"I won't need one of those thanks," Harry seemed miffed that he looked decrepit enough to need help with walking.

We then noticed that they were being handed to young and old alike.

"Well why don't you take one anyway, they're obviously handing them out to everyone."

Of course, as we walked up the extremely steep path of crumbling lava, even super-fit Harry had to admit that the stick came in handy. Once at the top, we knew that the climb had been worth the effort as we peered into the vast crater of that notorious volcano. To be there was a dream I'd had for many years. The Bay of Naples below us was shrouded in a blue mist. So beautiful, it almost took my breath away.

Eventually I had to be dragged away from the view, and making our way back down, we soon reached the exit gate. But the genial old character we expected to be awaiting the return of our sticks had been replaced by an altogether less benign presence. An old crone. Dressed entirely in black, she looked so much like the disguised Wicked Queen in *Disney*'s '*Snow White*', that I wouldn't have been surprised if she produced a large red apple from her pocket.

"Lire! Lire!" she cackled.

Terrified groups of young people in front of us were being harangued by this old witch for the 'hire' fee for those rustic sticks we'd believed to be part of the deal. Using her particular method of demanding money with menaces, there was probably quite a good living to be made out of the hundreds of foreign tourists passing through. Any person not being entirely familiar with the currency would easily be frightened into parting with large amounts of cash. She was onto a loser with us though.

"She's not having my supermarket trolley coin," I muttered under my breath with feeling. Shopping would have been difficult without that *cento* I'd been hanging onto for the past week or so.

Harry delved into his pockets and found a few remaining coins of even less value, and braving the tirade, dropped them into the outstretched bony hand. We then rushed through the gate while she shouted insults at our dust.

"Hope the old witch doesn't put a curse on us!" we laughed, as we skipped our care-free way back to the van.

We'd been driving back down for only a short distance when we caught up with a tourist bus. The road being narrow and with nowhere to pass, we trailed behind it for some distance, the school kids in the back waving at us until the novelty wore off. Approaching each bend, of which there seemed to be one every few yards, the coach had to stop and shunt backwards and forwards to get round. This type of manoeuvre seemed spookily similar to the way we had navigated ourselves into and out of the town of *Arcos de la Frontera* the previous year[2]. So instead of having a steady descent, we were obliged to stop and start. Eventually, we did manage to pass the coach, but almost immediately I sensed all was not well.

"Err, why are you pumping the brakes?"

"All that stopping hasn't done them any good."

Harry was calm, but I wasn't as I saw he was now resorting to the handbrake. This though was not proving very effective at slowing down a three and a half ton van. A nasty acrid burning smell hit my nose, smoke began to rise from somewhere underneath and it was clear that things were not as they should be. With no sign of any verges, lay-bys or side turnings, just the relentlessly steep road, I felt myself go hot and cold. I was panicking. *We were too young to die*. Then I realised that our guardian angel had looked after us long enough to reach safety. Here was the broad, prosperous-looking, tree-lined avenue I remembered having driven along earlier that day to get to Vesuvius. Either side of it were the entrances to driveways, along with wide grass and gravel verges. Harry steered us onto a verge under the shade of a tree.

Harry looked at me and grinned. "What's the matter? You're as white as a sheet!"

"Well, I wasn't keen on losing our brakes like that, in case you didn't guess." I replied.

"I was in control the whole time, you needn't have worried."

This coolness in a crisis was all very well, but on the odd occasion that he did show any sign of anxiety I might be led to think that we really were in trouble.

When the following year found us travelling to Italy via Switzerland, I was optimistic that all of the difficulties that had featured in our previous trips were behind us. Two shiny new batteries graced the engine compartment and expensive brake fluid had replaced the old cheap stuff put in by the previous owner. Harry was confident that we could now tackle any road without any problems. So confident that he was in favour of crossing the

Alps by the *Grand Saint Bernard* pass rather than the tunnel. I was reluctant.

"Think of all the beautiful scenery you'll miss. And the monastery. And we might even see the dogs. It'll be fine. Where's your sense of adventure?"

Where indeed.

In previous years we'd travelled by car using both methods. The tunnel had been jammed with lorries and you could hardly see a yard ahead for all the fumes. I loved the special atmosphere surrounding the Hospice of St Bernard. It was so remote yet people beat a path there. With that thought and on the off-chance of glimpsing one of those cute dogs, in the end I capitulated.

The way up the pass from *Martigny* was steep and rugged, but the van coped with it well. Forbidding, craggy black rocks form much of the Swiss side, and with long stretches never seeing much sunshine, you are left in no doubt that this is Northern Europe. Even though it was near the end of June, when we reached the high point of the Saint Bernard Hospice, the turquoise lake was frozen solid and huge banks of ploughed snow still lined both sides of the road. Mont Blanc shined in the distance, and the nearby slopes sparkled with the latest snow-fall. We stopped and absorbed the crystal air and the brilliant sunshine, but having a long way still to go that day our time there was limited.

All too soon, we began the descent towards Italy. The air began to feel warm and full of Mediterranean promise. *Puccini, Giotto, Brunelleschi, Michelangelo…*

The problem again seemed to result from getting stuck behind a slow moving vehicle. This time it was not a coach but a 'local', a small *Fiat* with a Turin number plate. The road was of course steep. Perhaps the driver was nervous, I know I would be, but to find an Italian driver who did not think he was *Fittipaldi* was unusual even on a mountain road. After following at this snail's pace for some time, it seemed like a good idea just to let him go and we pulled over to take in the scenery. Finding a place by a pretty stream and meadow, Harry sent our son and daughter a text message to tell them we were *"top of the world"*, a place they'd be familiar with from previous family holidays. This innocent act of texting would precede an emergency on more than one occasion.

With the *Vesuvius* experience still fresh in his mind, up till then Harry had been using the engine rather than the brakes to slow the van down. He didn't want to risk over-heating them despite the rejuvenated system. Soon after leaving our little idyll to continue the journey though, it became obvious that a large cloud of black smoke seemed to be following us.

"Oh no. Not again!" I wailed.

Rather than cause the engine more grief, Harry now decided to make more use of the brakes, but soon these too began to give out that familiar burning smell. He was now pumping the brake pedal and with smoke wafting from the wheels as well as the exhaust, I began to think that *déjà-vu* was becoming my middle name. This time though, it was worse. Being an alpine pass meant that the side which wasn't the mountain was a sheer drop, and there was nowhere else to go but down. I clung to the sides of the seat, although exactly what use this would be was not obvious. Harry put on the hazard warning lights and we made our precarious way down the road in a low gear, smoke seemingly coming from everywhere. After a while he pulled up at the side of the road to throw some of our precious water over the wheels to cool the brakes down. This caused an alarming hissing noise and a large cloud of steam, but at least it made a change from black smoke. With not much passing space, it was hazardous to stay where we were, so we limped on. Again our 'angel' flew by, and escorted us safely to an opening in the mountain-side where machinery and heaps of chippings etc. were being stored. We'd noticed a cheerful band of waving road menders further back and this must have been their base. An unlikely oasis, but it was good enough for us.

"I think we could do with a cup of tea!" Harry said cheerfully, in an effort to make light of the situation. I was shaking and also irrational.

"What if they want to get their machinery out of here?"

"For goodness' sake. You do worry about the most stupid things!"

Well that's what I'm like. There we were in a safe haven and all I could worry about was the remote possibility of being asked to move by some laid-back Italian workmen! Anyway, for the time being all was calm. I made tea, munched a *Hob Nob*, breathed in the mountain air and appreciated the view. After a while, Harry deemed the brakes also to have recovered enough to get on our way again, having thrown more water round the wheels to cool the area and tinkered about a bit, and we eventually set off.

"If there is a next time, *** the scenery, we'll use the tunnel," I mused as we passed the exit.

Those people emerging from it didn't know how lucky they were. They might have missed the best of the scenery, but they also had missed the character-forming experience of losing their brakes.

Our troubles were not completely over that day. Thankfully arriving at the first campsite after the tunnel, we soon discovered that our faithful electricity cable, having given sterling service in previous years, now decided to give up the ghost after less than a week's use. It was a while before Harry managed to sort it out and we could plug in: although it wasn't quite as simple as that. First he had the frustration of trying the usual contingent of dud power points around the site before finding one that actually was *live*.

The next morning the brakes seemed to be working perfectly and he decided that *Leyland Dafs'* braking systems were not designed with mountain roads in mind. Since *Daf* is a Dutch company, there could be a lot of truth in this – *terribly flat* Holland.

As a result of scaling the St. Bernard Pass, the engine was to give us problems throughout that trip, refusing to start each time until

Harry took the fuel filter to bits. This led to many delayed exits from campsites, lunch stops and supermarket car parks.

How I envied those people in smart new campervans.

"What on earth do they do to pass the time?" I wondered out loud.

"It must be so boring," my adventurous Other Half replied.

"I wish we could have a boring time."

The joint sigh of relief we always took upon arriving safely back on our side of the English Channel was no guarantee we'd seen the last of the difficulties of that particular trip. Once more, it was after texting our son and daughter that the trouble began. No sooner had BACK SAFELY IN UK… SPEAK SOON LOL M + D XX :-) flown out of the *Nokia* when a loud bang from the rear of the van followed by an awful flapping noise shocked us out of our complacency.

"What the hell was that?" I screamed.

Harry pulled onto the hard shoulder, although of course, of all places to have an emergency, this would have to happen on a flyover and therefore had not much in the way of one.

Braking down on the M20 was certainly the last thing I'd expected. Heavy traffic whizzed past us at 70 and over, there was an awful smell of diesel and even more worrying, what seemed like copious amounts of the stuff spreading around on the ground. And of course the light was fading fast.

With two pairs of rear wheels on the van, it was the tyre on one of these that had burst, damaging amongst other things the connection from the fuel filler to the tank. Luckily then, the diesel we could see was only the small amount still inside the pipe going between the two. It could have been far worse. I now knew at first hand how all those pieces of tyre one always saw on the sides of motorways had got there.

With the burst tyre being on the passenger side, Harry sorted out the jack and spare wheel and crawled under the van to carry out the wheel change.

"We could have called the AA," I suggested helpfully after he'd emerged from the nether regions.

"What about that huge bit of Gorgonzola in the fridge? By the time they turned up we'd have to dump it!" Why didn't I think ahead like he always did?

"And if they'd smelt that diesel, they'd have insisted on towing us off the motorway before they would touch the wheel." Never let it be said that food influences his decisions.

Once my hero had fixed the diesel pipe, we cautiously made our way to the nearest motorway service area. The famous cup of tea having been made and drunk, we were off again. Maybe one day our travels would be hitch free, but who wants everything to go smoothly? Well me, actually.

Oh, and for those also interested in food, the Gorgonzola did survive the trauma…

Notes
(1) See 'When in Rome'
(2) See 'Parable of a Parador'

An Arpeggio on the Campeggio

Those itty bitty Florentine pitches were never going to resemble U.S. ones, no matter how many olive trees they tried to mow down with their camper vans in the process.

It had all been so peaceful there on the *Campeggio Michelangelo* on its hillside above lovely *Firenze*. Having formed a little Anglo-Antipodean enclave in this haven just across the Arno, evenings were spent sitting outside our van at the end of each foot-sore but happy day in the city. Life in general and the day's site-seeing in particular were discussed over glasses of wine with our new Aussie and Kiwi friends, who had such an endearing and relaxed attitude to life, it was infectious. Screeching swallows and silent bats swooped overhead catching moths and what the Aussies term, 'mossies' in the darkening blue velvet sky. The lights of Florence began to twinkle below us, pale reflections of the bright stars above. Inhabitants of the *Campeggio Michelangelo* were busy with their evening meals and intriguing smells of food from different lands wafted over this microcosm of humanity. As though we were part of a *Fellini* film, that particular evening somewhere on site someone was practising the violin. Snatches of Bach's Double Violin Concerto drifted across the hillside, and sublime *arpeggios* provided the background music for our little soiree. Perfect harmony …

It was then that the reality of the world outside soon burst in on our modest scene of international concord. Two enormous motor caravans erupted into this special corner of Tuscany. The cliché 'bulls-in-a-china-shop' only just about covers it: this was just the prologue to the chaotic cartoon-like scene beginning to unfold before us.

Three different generations of Americans spilt out of these vans. If I described them as caricatures, that would be kind. The adults smoked, some were very fat and all were very loud. But it was the gross disrespect they had for the flora that really jarred. By repeatedly shunting the vans backwards and forwards, they attempted to enlarge each modestly-sized Florentine pitch into something of a more North American proportion, completely disregarding the damage being done to the ancient olive bushes forming the boundaries of each pitch. Even the shattering of one of the van windows by a tree branch having no right to be there in the first place, did not seem to deter them. Bemused onlookers, we sat with jaw-dropping, wide-eyed disbelief. Since each one of us possessed Anglo-Saxon genes, we were at great pains not to laugh out loud or make it too obvious we were watching this tasteless pantomime, but our new neighbours seemed oblivious to us anyway and unconcerned about the devastation they were causing.

Pop scratched his head and surveyed the scene. At last it had dawned on him that no matter how hard he and his wife (who was driving the other van) tried, those pesky little Italian pitches were not getting any bigger. They would all have problems trying not to roll out of bed later seeing as their overnight accommodation had been left standing at what can only be described as drunken angles.

As we sat there surreptitiously watching from behind our glasses of wine, not daring to look each other in the eye, Grandma and Mom produced chairs far too small for their generously sized rear ends and proceeded to sit chain smoking in the middle of the roadway.

"Y'all play nicely!" they yelled at the kids, who were now screeching and hitting each other with tennis racquets.

Meanwhile, Pop swanned around like a Texan oil baron wearing a Stetson and puffing on a huge cigar as though he owned the place.

"Aw! Leave 'em alone Mildred. They're jus' havin' fun," he bellowed.

Fellini had been replaced by the *Jerry Springer Show*. That night we discovered it was possible to be horrified, annoyed and amused all at the same time, in much the same way as Springer's audience are I guess.

The following morning they set off *en masse,* and with difficulty pushed Grandma in a wheelchair up the slopes of the site, presumably to spend the day in Florence. It was about 10.30. We planned to leave that day, but as the pitch was ours until one o'clock, before our departure we decided to visit the beautiful little jewellery-box Romanesque church of *San Miniato al Monte*, only a short walk further up the *Viale Michelangelo*. When we returned at about 12.45, Mildred and co. were paying at the reception before relieving the site of their presence. So much mayhem for such a short stay. They'd certainly made an impression on the place in more ways than one. That national stereotypes can be formed so easily by one unfortunate example was patently clear.

But fortunately for international relations, our travels round Italy brought us into contact with many shining representatives of young people from that same land, who went a long way to compensate for the brash behaviour of their compatriots. The exquisite Peggy Guggenheim museum in Venice was a large factor in restoring our good opinion. Side by side with the amazing collection of both famous and less well-known quirky modern works, is a staff of bright young American college students on a year's attachment to the gallery. They were a breath of fresh air. Appreciating their privileged position in incredible Venice, they couldn't have been more helpful and friendly.

Our van, as may have been gathered already, may not have been exactly state of the art, but it was very clean and up together, containing most of the essentials needed for quite a comfortable few weeks of travelling. By comparison, the many intrepid young travellers we encountered, mostly from Australia and New Zealand, were not so well endowed on the mod-cons front. Before returning to their homes in the Southern hemisphere and real life, they would be spending months at a time bumming round Europe in beaten up, rusting camper-vans, usually elderly Volkswagens. These VW campers may be quite trendy, but are also quite small with only enough space inside for not much more than a bed, let alone any toilet facilities. Some may contain a small 'fridge, but the male occupant of such a vehicle wouldn't give a *Four X* for chilling anything other than his 'tinnies' in it, leaving any female travelling companion the problem of stopping the milk from going off. The combination of vintage and neglect means that these vehicles are prone to major mechanical problems, making most of our episodes seem quite mild in comparison.

At the root of all these difficulties lies the continuous recycling of camper-vans amongst the Antipodean ex-pat community in London. We discovered that with each European trip completed, they i.e. the vans rather than the sellers, are parked along a certain road in the capital to be sold on to the next intrepid bunch of trekkers. The new owners' enthusiasm for their forthcoming trip blinds them to the fact that they've acquired an unroadworthy wreck. One wondered if details such as MOT inspections are conveniently forgotten about since the vans did not spend a lot of time on British roads. Consequently each new owner, usually a young professional with more knowledge of the mechanics of the world economy than that of an engine, experiences a string of break-downs all over Europe. Hence they become fodder for many an unscrupulous foreign motor mechanic. But despite the stop-start nature of their travels, things never seemed to get them down.

This knowledge of the workings of the campervan recycling scheme we gained from the young Aussie couple we'd set up next to on the *Campeggio Michelangelo*. They had endured numerous problems with their VW during an extensive trip around Europe. For example, while in Spain, realising that the oil light had been flashing for some time, they eventually decided that they should perhaps top up the engine with oil at the next service station. Before they got that far however, the engine seized up, with a costly replacement the inevitable outcome.

"No worries, mate!"

Despite knowing they'd been ripped off by the garage involved, they remained cheerful and optimistic. 'Easy-going' seemed to be the default character setting for every Aussie and New Zealander we met during our travels.

Our timing that year in Florence was just right, for we'd arrived there as it was preparing to celebrate its Saint's day. The festival for *San Giovanni* culminates with fireworks being let off from the *Piazzale Michelangelo* just a very short walk up the road from the campsite on the *Viale Michelangelo*, so I was thrilled that for once we had actually managed to be in the right place at the right time. It always seems that we are fated to coincide our arrival anywhere with the day after some amazing annual extravaganza has taken place or a never-to-be repeated art exhibition etc. had finished. We've also been known to arrive simultaneously too early and too late, such as when we tried to visit the Matisse Museum in his native town of *Le Catau* in Northern France, only to find the building roofless and in the process of extensive renovations which would not be completed until the following year. But that year in Florence, we were in luck.

Living near Cowes, the renowned centre of the yachting world, we've become *blasé* about the dazzling firework displays outside the harbour at the close of the annual *'Cowes Week'* regatta. With this in mind, we could be forgiven for not finding fireworks as thrilling as we might, but *au contraire*. To have one of the world's most beautiful Renaissance city's as a backdrop for the display made Cowes harbour seem as dull as a muddy puddle, despite its pastel-painted cottages, bobbing yachts and narrow, bunting festooned streets. Perhaps too it was the novelty of watching such a display on a dry, warm and still evening that helped, something of a rarity during the first week of August in Cowes, although it has been known. But my over-riding memory of that evening is of stars exploding above the cool and serene head of Michelangelo's statue of *David,* who ignored the spectacular as he gazed out thoughtfully over the city.

When it came to intrepid travellers, it was not just the under thirties who qualified. We were staying overnight on a coastal site to the north of Rome, amusingly and no doubt innocently named 'Camping Queen', when a thin and frail-looking man, long past his youth, arrived on a bicycle and set up an impossibly minute tent. As the sole inhabitants of the small touring area, the rest of the place being fairly deserted and consisting of the usual numerous 'permanent' tents, we were soon in conversation with our new neighbour. He'd just flown in from New Zealand where he lived, although was Dutch in origin.

"I'm cycling to Cambridge", he told us, as though it was the most normal thing in the world to do: ride there on a bike from Rome.

That we were amazed was an understatement.

"My wife's from there," he went on, "and she's going meet me there."

"Is there any special reason you're doing this?" I asked tentatively.

"Just an ambition," he calmly replied. "Err, is there a kitchen here?"

"No, not as far as we know,"

"Only in New Zealand all the campsites have kitchens, you see. I was expecting the same in Europe,"

Well if there was a site with such facilities in France, Spain or Italy, we'd yet to come across it.

"I'll just have to get a takeaway then!" he laughed.

The *Camping Queen* wasn't far up the road from one of Rome's suburbs, but I couldn't help but be concerned. He had no equipment other than a tiny Primus stove, which would take an age to boil even a small mug of water, so later we made him a cup of tea, and the next morning Harry also made him coffee. It was the least we could do. I was feeling quite guilty about wallowing in the relative luxury of our van, with its loo compartment, 'fridge and cooker.

To make matters worse, he later told us his planned route through the Alps to France.

"I'm hoping to travel through the Mont Blanc Tunnel."

Oh my God! The thought of him pedalling through that juggernaut infested, fume-filled hell-hole was shocking.

Harry and I looked at each other. "I'm not too sure if you can actually go through on a bike,"

Not only was the tunnel horrendous, but the gruelling, narrow pass up to it was as bad.

When we left for Rome the next day, we wished him luck as he packed all his worldly goods into the pannier of his bike. Did he make it to Cambridge? We would never know. Only a few people had email then, and it seemed intrusive to ask for his address. I spent the next couple of weeks pondering his fate.

How people end up where they do is often a source for conjecture. Having just arrived on a site near Allessandria and it being early afternoon, all was quiet and peaceful with only the gentle breeze in the trees and cries from passing overhead birds breaking the silence. As we sat outside enjoying a cool beer and looking forward to restful couple of hours of tranquillity, a rather large and somewhat dishevelled lady of mature vintage ambled past us. Pushing a ramshackle bicycle and leading a pathetic and mangy-looking mongrel on a piece of string, she would have looked more at home in a cardboard box on a London street than on an Italian campsite.

"I noticed your number plate and thought I'd say hello,"

We didn't mind at first, as a bit of English conversation with someone we were not married to, was welcome once in a while. It didn't take much encouragement on our behalf for her to impart her life story, telling us that she had lived in various parts of Italy for some time, wrote children's books (though obviously without much remuneration) and was now staying 'semi-permanently' on the site. She had family elsewhere, but it sounded suspiciously like they'd dumped her on this campsite to get her out of their hair. Luckily for them though, she still had a mission in life.

"I'm trying to get them to eradicate the mosquitoes here,"

Well there were a few around going by the nets outside the chalets dotted round the site.

"They breed in the drainage ditch," she went on," I keep putting salt down, but it's not enough. I've taken it up with the owners, but they're not interested."

"What they really need to do is spray the whole place with insecticide. I can get my son to do it. He's a pilot and will be more than willing if they'd only let him."

She failed to see why anyone would object to this, but in the interests of harmony we demurred from saying anything either way and made all the right sympathetic noises. This solution was obviously full of hazards for everyone in the area, not to mention the fantastic wild life that abounded in those parts. Still, it takes all sorts, and if the campaign gave her an interest in life, why should we put a dampener on it.

This lady occupied a big chunk of what we had hoped would be our relaxing afternoon, and we assumed that because the site was not exactly on the main tourist route, she'd been starved of the company of English-speakers for some time. Before eventually tearing herself away from our fascinating company, she imparted some interesting news about that evening's on-site entertainment.

"Are you going to the Celtic evening here?" she asked. "The Major's coming,"

We hadn't seen the posters but it sounded interesting.

Being a big fan of *Riverdance* and such-like, I was quite excited about this. It did seem a little incongruous that this type of music was to be played in the heart if the Italian countryside, but there-again, it was no different to South American pan pipes in the plaza at Covent Garden.

There was an air of expectation as the start of the concert approached, with a large contingent of locals, including the town's mayor, gathering for the show. The children's play area, near to where we'd set up home that afternoon, had been turned into an open air venue with a stage and seating, and as the sky darkened and the bats swooped overhead, the band began to play. Even though the musicians turned out to be Italians rather than Celts, Scottish reels and Irish jigs soon filled the night air. *Riverdance* had become an international sensation, following that amazing performance during the then recent Dublin Eurovision Song Contest, and Irish music and dance was making a comeback as a consequence. We stood at the back, my feet itching to dance, and like Moira Shearer in the *Red Shoes*, I was having difficulty keeping still. It was disappointing to realise though that the rest of the audience seemed clamped motionless in their seats like a pious church congregation. They were not even tapping their feet or beating time with or on any other part of their anatomy. I turned to Harry.

"If this performance was anywhere in the UK, people would be up dancing by now,"

"Well why don't you start them off?"

"I think I'll pass, on that suggestion thank you."

The end of each piece was greeted by restrained and polite applause rather than the American-style whoops and shouts which we've become accustomed to. It was so surprising that this popular folk music seemed to leave the warm-blooded Italians cold. I was disappointed. The British are meant to be reserved. What was it the Latino soul didn't get?

Despite this low-key reception, I was enjoying the concert. Not all the pieces played had lyrics, but those that did were sung in a strange tongue we assumed to be Gaelic but may well have been English with a strong Italian accent. This must have been why we didn't realise immediately that we were being entertained with a song extolling the virtues of the IRA. The 'Troubles' were not really a thing of the past at that time, and it all began to feel a little uncomfortable, so we decided it was time to take our leave. If my evening of uplifting Celtic music had turned out to be a little joyless, this completed the picture.

I'd never been to an Irish wake, but I now had more of an idea what it would be like.

No Woman No Cry   Attractive scaffolding at *Puçol*

No Woman No Cry The loneliness of the early-season traveller

Parable of a Parador   *Arcos de le Frontera*
The Parador - How do we get up there?

Parable of a Parador
Arcos de la Frontera View from the Parador Terrace

Allie Sommerville

Parable of a Parador   How on earth did we get through this arch, and up to the Parador? (And I'm only 5 feet tall!)

Parable of a Parador   The view from our room

Parable of a Parador
The Plaza at *Arcos* with the Parador to the right, our van in the centre and the 'picturesquely crumbling' Baroque Church to the left.

Parable of a Parador We get the feeling that the way down may be a bit trickier than the way up…

Inauguration of the Innocent   Evening exertions

On How to Find…a Campsite
Outside cheerfully named *Camping CalaGoGo, El Prat de Llobregat, Barcelona*

Allie Sommerville

On How to Find a Campsite…
Alcalá del Júcar – We were almost in it before we saw it

On How to Find a Campsite Picturesque and well-hidden
Alcalá del Júcar

On How to Find...*Alcalá del Júcar* – bridge over the *Rio Júcar*

On How to Find...Relaxing on the peaceful mountain site found by chance at *Villares* near *Córdoba*

"...we've got a problem..."
Le Col Grande St. Bernard under snow still in June

"...we've got a problem..."
Thankful to make it across the Alps after the brakes failed

"...we've got a problem..." At the crater of Vesuvius – my Other Half doesn't look like he needed that stick!

An Arpeggio on the Campeggio
Our Aussie 'Neighbours' in Florence – VW in the background

Noises Off All is calm on that *Pyrénéenne* site when we arrive

Noises Off
Flat back four on the football pitch but at least it's quiet

More Noises and Other Nuisances...*Chanticleer* and his harem – quiet here but we could have wrung his neck at 4.00am

Allie Sommerville

A Hitch-Hiker Guides…to Montserrat 'Our' car park in the distance, suspended over the cliff and now filled with coaches

A Hitch-Hiker Guides…to Montserrat   Dancers in the square

When in Rome   Suitably dressed for St. Peter?

Allie Sommerville

Shouting in the Sistine   A Nun's Story

Money, Money, Money
We didn't descend from the *Puy de Dôme* like this!

Money, Money, Money
The *Puy de Dôme* after our more conventional descent

Venice – Vaporetti and Victimisation... The *vaporetto* station at the *Rialto* where we 'lost' our would-be house-guest

Apes Rocks & Pizza – *San Roque* from Gibraltar
Our van is out there somewhere on the Spanish perimeter road

Apes Rocks & Pizza – Gibraltar   "Behind you!"

Allie Sommerville

Apes Rocks & Pizza   The *faro* of *Trafalgar*

Fuentes! Some want to get wet while others can't stay dry

Fuentes! Happy band of damp pilgrims

Fuentes!
Chopping wood on the ancient Roman aqueduct at *Segovia* – Laurie Lee stayed at an inn under the arches, but we didn't find it, unsurprisingly

Top Ten Tips
Utilising some of the items mentioned, at the surprisingly peaceful site next to the *Monza* motor-racing circuit near *Milano*

I love Italy
In *Parma* - armed as usual with a guidebook

Noises Off...

If there were a championship in talking, Spain would not need to look far for their entrant. He is there, still droning on at that campsite in the Pyrenees. I'm sure I can hear him.

It was our début on a Spanish campsite and we were unprepared for what lay in store. We'd arrived at the first one across the border in early afternoon. How peaceful it all seemed with the air warm and fragrant and nothing to be heard apart from the screech of buzzards wheeling above us on the thermals. After booking in, a nice young man on a Lambretta was to lead us to our pitch.

It was all a bit strange. The site was built on a hill and crammed onto every tier were shanty-like dwellings. Not at all what we had expected in the vast spaces which the southern slopes of the Pyrennées provided, but we followed wide-eyed and hoping for something better when it came to our place in the scheme of things.

We looked at each other, "Where is everyone?"

Well maybe people only come here on weekends we agreed. We chose to ignore the fact that even though empty, numerous cars and kids bikes and toys littered the place, and lines of washing were strung around the tents and static caravans like bunting at a street party. It looked like there'd been a bomb scare or the body snatchers had paid a visit.

"Well this is fantastic anyway!" I said, not caring at all why the place was deserted.

"Did you see the pool?" my daughter at that age rarely enthused about anything except footballers. "I just can't wait to jump in!"

There was an incredible view of the mountains, a hot Mediterranean sun shining and the large swimming pool shimmered beneath it. Having the luxury of a pool to ourselves was too much of a temptation to avoid and we put all the things we should have been doing on arrival onto the back-burner. However, as the afternoon wore on, we gradually became aware of a general buzz creeping over the place like an approaching swarm of bees. By night-time, like *Jeckyl and Hyde*, the site completely changed its character The sleeping giant had awoken refreshed and was ready to party. Hundreds of people began milling about but there was a happy, laid-back family atmosphere and we loved it.

We walked along by the river that flowed next to the site, and it was pleasant to see boys and their dads quietly trailing fishing lines across the gently rippling water whilst other groups of youngsters were enjoying themselves by larking about along the bank. Without thinking, Harry skimmed a stone across the surface, as is his wont whenever he comes to any expanse of water. This seemed to be an unusual skill in those parts, because immediately he was surrounded by an entourage of young admirers, who urged him to show them how to achieve this incredible feat – a stone bouncing on water!

"I don't think those people fishing quite appreciated you passing on that particular bit of British expertise," I suggested.

"Oops! Didn't think of that!"

I thought it prudent that we should hurry on and leave the apprentice skimmers to practise their newly acquired art without further tuition. I have the feeling that we may have started an unfortunate craze.

This being our first night in Spain, it was a great novelty to walk around in the warm night air listening to the strange to us sounds of the Catalan language all around. To complete the soundscape though, it was not traditional music reaching our ears but the familiar sound of the theme for *'East Enders'*. The TV room was full of teenagers avidly watching an episode from the soap screened some time before in the UK, when I had been a regular follower, (much too depressing now). We found it hilarious to hear the dubbed on Spanish voices of *'Dirty Den'* and his wife *'Ange'*, the original main characters of the soap. *'Ange'* had the most deliciously deep, latino *femme fatale* voice in complete contrast to the normally shrill 'East End' tones of the actress Anita Dobson who played her. Here, I am shocked to say that Harry, having already ruined the evening pastime of one set of people, then went on to give away the soap's future plot-line to these Spanish teenagers.

"The hombre," he joked, "*finito*," and here he ran his hand across his throat in a theatrical gesture of murder. There were gasps all round, but at least they could boast to their friends at home that they knew what was going to happen in future episodes.

When we eventually returned to the 'van it was quite late, even for us, so we were ready to settle down for the night after what had been a long and tiring day with all the travelling, swimming, eating and drinking. At that time, our only experience of campsites had been on the drive down through France, where fellow travellers were either British or from other northern countries of Europe, such as the Netherlands, Belgium and Germany. Whilst staying on these sites, we discovered that as was usual in most aspects of life, we seemed to be out of step with everyone else. We were always the last to put out our lights at night and the latest to emerge in the mornings. In Spain, we were still at odds with everyone: it soon became clear that we fell somewhere between the two factions of early birds and night owls.

It was disconcerting to find no one else on the site at that late hour was at all interested in sleep. If anything, the volume of noise was increasing. Dozens of TV's blared out a multitude of different channels, while loud pop music was broadcast from large ghetto blasters, babies cried for attention and children still played wild games outside.

Rising above all the noise, adults were conducting arguments, though as we'd discovered from previous trips to Continental Europe, they were probably only having a chat. But amazingly, through all this din, one voice managed to outstrip everything and emerge triumphantly as a force of its own. A deep and lugubrious drone was coming from the tent adjacent to us. Its perpetrator did not even seem to pause for breath. Who knows what he found to hold forth on, but he held sway over his tented audience like some Bedouin potentate. Although there were plenty of other people in there, it was only his voice we could hear. Maybe no-one was actually listening to what he had to say, but unfortunately, his enclave being right next to us, we had no choice but to listen as we lay there trying to get some sleep.

We all tried unison shouting, "Shut Up!" but this made no difference. With the voice having wormed its way into our brains like a hideous parasite, it was as if someone was banging a bass drum inside our heads.

After what seemed like hours of this torture, exasperated, nerves frayed by lack of sleep, Harry jumped out of bed, threw on some clothes, unhooked the electricity and drove us away from the Catalonian motormouth. In the dark we didn't know where we had ended up, but the main thing was that we were away from the monotonous prattle. If we thought we could now settle down for some rest though, we were wrong. In the way that an annoying and much detested song gets into your head and you find yourself unable to shift it for days, we were stuck with *his master's voice*. Despite the distance now between us making it impossible, we could still hear him. The gods however hadn't finished with us for the night, because soon we were shaken by a terrific thunderstorm and torrential downpour. At least it served to drown out the reverberations left inside our ears.

Peeping out of the windows the following morning, we found ourselves to be the flat back four in an extremely muddy football field, but it could have been worse. Tents pitched nearer to the river were now under a foot of water and we felt sorry for these people wringing out their sleeping bags, even if they had been partly responsible for the cacophony of the previous night. Those away from the flood were of course still yet to emerge after their exertions into the small hours.

Although it was not exactly early when we left, we felt sure that we ought to be particularly quiet when we passed the encampment of our former neighbour. After all, at that hour the poor soul could have had only a few hours sleep himself. What a shame then that we had to rev the engine on our van to get up the slope that passed his tent.

Notes (1) see Inauguration of the Innocents

…More Noises
…and other nuisances

Imagine the scene: it is summer in a small hamlet in the heart of the French countryside. All is peaceful and idyllic…

…well it can be, but living in the English equivalent has made us a little cynical of this romantic perception of the pastoral life. The inner city must be quieter than our road. Everyday country activities such as muck-spreading, silaging and harvesting, means that all manner of farm machinery trundles up and down adjacent fields or tears past our house Schumacher-style. Add to this the routine summer morning dash to the nearest sandy beach by inmates of the local holiday camp, and we might as well be under the Heathrow flight-path.

It was whilst staying at a friend's *gite* in a small and picturesque *village fleurie* in Northern France, we realised that the road *chez nous* didn't quite have the monopoly on bucolic aggravations. Local *fermiers* in their spanking new and no doubt expensively subsidised tractors, spent the day whizzing up and down the narrow and inadequately pavemented street outside, shaking us out of our seats on a regular basis. The parasoled tables and chairs outside a charming little café opposite were regularly scattered as if by a tornado, resulting in a *Looney Tunes* sequence of the red-faced, moustachioed proprietor chasing after these drivers wielding a meat cleaver.

Despite having no illusions about country life, this didn't prevent us from being optimistic about finding a quiet stopping place for our van during our travels. But it didn't take long for reality to bite. The usual suspects indicted with breaching the campsite peace were: church bells, chiming clocks, dogs, cockerels, busy roads and railways. In addition to these common-place nuisances though, firing ranges, wedding parties, disco's, 'fetes', pile-driving, road-laying and even air-force display teams added to the rich mix of annoyances.

While Spain was the worst place for dogs barking through the night, the Pyrenees took the prize for chiming clocks. There they insist on striking the hour five minutes before, on the hour and five minutes after. Well at least you didn't have to look at your watch to find out how much longer you had to lay there without sleep.

The site at the grandly named *Nouan le Fuselier* in the *Sologne* region of France enabled us to tick off all but one of the common nuisances. On arrival we'd detected none. It was only after installing ourselves with electricity, outdoor table and chairs, glass of wine etc., that we began to tune in to the intruders on that otherwise lovely location. In addition to these, that horrendous but almost silent enemy of the camper, the gnat, was especially prolific. Having unfortunately already paid in advance, we applied the spray liberally, poured out more wine and stoically attempted to ignore all those noises off and those other nuisances.

Even arriving early at a campsite and therefore spending the best part of a day there before nightfall, did not guarantee full knowledge of its disadvantages in the noise department.

Of those places we discovered by chance, lovely *Rhinau*, next to the Rhine in the *Alsace*, was one of the best. The campsite, part of a farm, was spacious, its owners welcoming, and above all it was quiet. There was also a very nice swimming pool and even smoking was banned in the sparking lavatory blocks. The usual things that plagued us noise-wise were absent: the hours were marked without the sound of chiming clocks or church bells, no dogs barked at imagined menaces. In fact it all seemed pretty much perfect. On arrival, the friendly owner had advised us that their village *fête* was to be held that night in the café area on the site, and she hoped that the music would not disturb us. Always the one for a bit of local colour, I asked what kind of music, but the answer I received was a bit vague.

"Oh, our usual *musique*," she told me.

"Sounds promising," I thought optimistically.

She assured us that the festivities would finish at or not long after midnight,

"Minuit peut-être, ou minuit et demi,"

As we are not in the habit of retiring early, this was no problem. I was quite looking forward to a bit of *Alsacian* 'atmosphere'.

Our pitch had the advantage of being specially designed with hard standing for camper vans, and was next to a large hen run. The hen 'house' was a picturesquely crumbling barn attached to the main farmhouse. This did not seem to be any problem, since the run did not emit any untoward smells and the antics of the hens and their vigilant and swaggering cockerel boss provided a source of entertainment. Along with most of the children on the site, we amused ourselves by feeding our feathered neighbours with various delicacies, assessing their preferences for each. Well one has to do something to pass the time.

Evening arrived, and the good folk of *Rhinau* gathered for their '*fête*'. The party was obviously going with a swing because eating, singing and dancing was still a force to be reckoned with when even we settled down for the night. We assumed someone would call a halt to the proceedings before too long, because after all, hadn't we been assured that it would stop at half past midnight at the latest?

At three a.m. however, things were still as animated as an *Ibizan* nightclub, and we were becoming just a bit put out about this. Nowhere nearly as put out though as our Belgian neighbours. They voted with their wheels, packed up and drove off at this unearthly hour presumably to find a bit of peace away from *Rhinau*. The sound of other people enjoying themselves at a party you haven't been invited to can be very annoying, and even ear plugs weren't effective barriers against all the racket. Eventually, and following several franglicised karaoke renditions of *'My Way'* (unfortunately, my wish for authentic folk-song had long been given up as this represented the fête's play list) followed by a strangely-worded attempt at *Auld Lang Syne,* the revellers took their leave; trying to do so as quietly as they possibly could in an inebriated state. Which of course was not very quiet at all.

If we now thought we at least had a few hours left before the site once more sprang to life, we did not have long to think again. Just before dawn, which after all was only a very short time following the departure of the last reveller, *Chanticleer* decided to greet the new day. Even though he had kept us amused the previous day, all that was forgotten with the sound of that first 'cock-a-doodle-doo'.

Ironically, soon after our arrival we'd liked the place so much that we decided to stop there for a few days. Though we knew the party was a one-off, the early morning alarm call was no encouragement to prolong our stay. We decided to approach the owner.

"Is it possible to have a place away from the chicken run?"

She clapped her hands to her face, *"Le coq! Je suis desolée!"*

"Usually I lock 'im up in ze barn, but was very late when I come to bed last night," she explained unnecessarily.

" 'E will not make noise if 'e in barn," she went on, "I was not my usual self last night,"

She certainly wasn't if it had been her singing *"My Way"*.

So we decided to remain neighbours to the *poulets*, but still ended up moving our van to another pitch. After the Belgians had done their moonlight flit, next morning they were replaced by a Danish couple. Our new neighbours spent the whole time sitting outside their van chain-smoking. I felt like screaming. Here we were in an almost perfect place, but still things were being sent to annoy us.

Railways often figured in nuisance value on many sites throughout Spain and Italy, but France didn't escape entirely. Luckily though, in many places there, the sound of trains is only heard as a distant rumble, unless it's the *TGV*, when it's more of a distant roar. Elsewhere unfortunately, the distances involved are about as far as I can throw a stone, which is not far at all.

Franco's striving for economic success before tourism took off, was concentrated on the Mediterranean coast, now such a magnet for Northern European sun seekers. With amazing foresight, he constructed the railway linking the heavy industries to run right next to, and parallel with, its beaches. Of course then they were mere landing places for fishing boats. As Laurie Lee put it:

"*...one could have bought the whole coast for a shilling. Not Emperors could buy it now*"[1].

The one site in Spain which fulfilled my idealistic hope of camping right on the beach, also therefore had this railway literally running through it. Access from one part to the other was gained through a tunnel under the track, and the trains ran all night. Not quite utopia.

Another attraction of the beaches along this coast does not relate to noise. Instead, the chemical or steel works alluded to before, are often conveniently located in order that the cheerfully lurid colours of their outflows contribute a picturesque dimension to the beach scene. Add to this the unusual aroma also being emitted and you can see that we just had to tear ourselves away from such inviting places.

A good place for keen train-spotters was at the town of *Casino* in Italy, set beneath the monastery at *Montecasino*, the scene of a devastating battle during the Second World War.

We'd had the usual frustrating tour of the town following signs for its elusive campsite. When at last we found it, the place was closed. In fact it looked as if *Garibaldi* and his followers had been the last occupants. If a dead crow and a skeleton were swinging from this gate it wouldn't have been surprising. The only thing giving it a slight footing in the present was the familiar sight of the flags of all nations above the entrance gate. Once they had welcomed visitors, but when we found them, they were shredded and flapping like the 'colours' of a regiment hanging in a church to commemorate victory in a long forgotten battle.

Giving up on that one then, we did eventually find nearby something described as 'Parking' for camper vans. It was a very small site, but pleasant enough, incredibly cheap, with a very kind lady running it. The area to set up on had lovely lush newly mown grass, useful for Harry to lay underneath the van on to fix yet another thing that had gone wrong. There was also the luxury of pristine 'hotel-style' individual washrooms. Sounds perfect? It might have been if the place wasn't immediately next to the main north-south railway line. Metallic monsters rattled the van and our nerves continuously throughout the night.

There is peace out there somewhere. I just know there is.

Notes (1) As I walked out One Midsummer Morning – Laurie Lee

A Hitch-Hiker Guides …to Montserrat

"Are you heading for a campsite at Montserrat?" we asked hopefully.

That huge rucksack was large enough to hold enough tent accommodation for a family of six, so we seemed to be onto a sure bet that there was somewhere to pitch it.

"Yes, sure. Can you give me a lift please?" the hitchhiker replied in impeccable English.

She was a pleasant young local, and chatted easily to us during the journey. Despite Manchester United having recently beaten nearby Barcelona's team in some cup or other, luckily everyone had behaved themselves, so she was inclined to be friendly towards us Brits. However, I couldn't help noticing that as we got nearer to our destination, she became a little evasive about the alluded-to campsite, and I tried to pin her down on the details of where to find it.

"Are there directions to the campsite when we get there?" I probed.

"Oh well, I'm not certain," she now looked embarrassed. "I'm not *exactly* sure if there is anything other than for tents really."

Harry and I exchanged glances. He suspected, as I did, that she knew all along there was nowhere for campervans and the like up at *Montserrat*. If she'd revealed this straight away, she might have waved goodbye to the lift. We were committed by then. It was becoming too late to go all of the way back down to find somewhere else to stay overnight, so we continued onwards and upwards with hope in our hearts.

Now this sort of thing wouldn't have happened if we'd planned our journeys down to the last detail. But this is not really our style. Because we never knew how long it would take to get anywhere in our van and what other distractions might tempt us away from our chosen path, there seemed little point in deciding everything before setting off. Not for us the boringly sensible action of pre-booking anywhere to stop overnight. Left to my own devices, I would be much in favour of such practical proceedings. While Harry is more adventurous I would on the whole rather do without any adventures at all. Adventure means worry, and the hair-colouring is having enough problems covering up the grey. Travelling round as free agents is definitely not for the faint-hearted, so I just had to grin, bear it and keep my fingers crossed.

Despite all the anxious moments created by this footloose attitude, I begrudgingly admit to there being an up side. Unintentional deviations, popularly known as taking a wrong turn or getting lost, things which occurred on a regular basis, were usually compensated with an amazing view or a fascinating piece of local 'colour'. Sometimes both. You can imagine how enriched we were by all that compensation. Spending the night near the monastery at *Montserrat*, is a good example of how this works. Of course we hadn't actually planned to stay in a car park.

Being astonished by *Gaudi*'s architectural wonders in the searing heat of the Catalonian capital made us hanker for somewhere cool and calm. Although our guidebook showed a magnificent aerial photo of the monastery at *Montserrat*, it gave little actual information about the place, but as it was away from the city and moreover on top of a mountain it looked like it fitted the bill perfectly. Unfortunately, our Spanish *'Mapa de Campings'* did not indicate a campsite there, but we weren't unduly worried because this map was as yet untried. It turned out later not exactly to be much use at all. The words 'chocolate' and 'fireguard' sprung to mind in connection with this marvellous publication, since even those places that **were** shown had proved impossible to find. Still, it was free. As long as we could find the road up the mountain though, all would be well...

Unfortunately, by this time Barcelona had begun its rush hour enabling us to discover some of the less salubrious quarters of the city as we were swept along with the tide. Barcelona, in common with all other large cities, is full of drivers familiar with the layout, who know exactly where they are going and are intent on getting there as quickly as possible. Any strangers in town fall victim to this madness, and are carried on the current like spiders down a drain, to places which they really had no intention of going to, and getting there, usually wished they hadn't. Fortunately a stray wave washed us into the road tunnel beneath the mountain, direction, *Montserrat*. As the Spanish sun began to draw its *"curtains of blood"*[1] it was reassuring that we were now heading in the right direction.

Finding a campsite in Spain, in the daylight, is hard enough even when you **know** there is definitely one nearby. Once it's dark you may as well forget it. Hoping that we might have the luck to come across one without actually knowing of its existence seemed like a long shot, but we were used to that. At dusk, the road up that mountain seemed endless, with steep hairpin bends every few yards, at each of which we had to stop to let a coach pass coming down from the other direction.

It was some distance along this torturous uphill struggle that we noticed the young woman hitchhiking and decided this was the perfect opportunity to find out if we were on a hiding to nothing. Following our awkward questions, the conversation with our guest began to stall, but luckily for her, the road finally stopped winding. We could see in front of us the small village below the monastery, though it was puzzling to find barriers across the road to gain access to it and the enormous car park immediately ahead. Our guest seemed familiar with all of this and told us just to take a ticket from the machine, and as though entering our local super-market car park, the barrier lifted to allow us through. She thanked us, we said our goodbyes and despite her heavy load, she disappeared with what could only be described as excessively deliberate haste, into a noisy, milling throng of similarly equipped young people.

As there was no obvious road that might lead us to the hoped-for campsite, we left the van on one of the huge car parks (there was more than one) and made our way into the village to make inquiries at the tourist office. Our suspicions had been right. The only casual accommodation at Montserrat consisted of a couple of back-packers' huts at the summit of the mountain and a youth hostel in the village. However on the plus side, we'd noticed a rather nice looking three star hotel in the pretty village square, and to stay there would be a welcome break from spending the night in the van. We reasoned that the place wouldn't be that busy as it was such a pain to get to, and even though it was a Saturday, it was after all early in the season. The car parks were empty and there were few people about once those back-packers had disappeared. It was a sure thing no-one else would be after accommodation that night. We entered the cosy reception area and were greeted by a very friendly receptionist.

"We'd like to book a room for the night," I ventured confidently.

"Lo siento, madame. We have no rooms."

"Nothing? Nothing at all?"

We were amazed that despite all appearances, there was no room for us at the inn. But all was still not hopeless.

"There is a room in the pension next door. Maybe you would like this?"

He sounded doubtful, but I assumed that the slight rise at the end of the sentence may have been picked up through watching too many Australian soaps in an attempt to learn English. He handed us a key, the huge size and antiquity of which should have told us something straight away. We left the reception and headed for the pension, an innocent enough, white-painted building attached to the side of the hotel.

Stepping into the entrance corridor of this building was like entering the seedy set of a 1930s, black and white 'film noire' movie. The vogue for trendy interior decoration had obviously completely passed this place by. It couldn't have seen as much as a pot of paint in decades. Worn linoleum covered the floor, everywhere was dark and dingy and with two inch gaps under the doors of the guestrooms, it wasn't exactly The Ritz. 'Our' room was on the second floor, but on entering it, we became even more horrified. A shabby iron bedstead was illuminated by a single unshaded 20 watt bulb, lighting it seemed specially designed to complete the ambience. The atmosphere was so sinister it wouldn't have been too surprising if *Peter Lorrie* had rushed out from one of the other rooms into that gloomy corridor, leaving his hapless victim stretched out lifeless on another of those horrible iron bedsteads. We seemed to have entered the *Twilight Zone*, and with my flesh creeping and my imagination in its habitual state of overdrive, I couldn't get out of there quick enough.

When we returned the key, I felt sure that I saw the original receptionist go into hiding in a back office, embarrassed he'd thought for one second that we would be interested in that lovely room. The man now at the desk, although looking a little sheepish, did not seem at all surprised that we'd passed up the offer of such enticing accommodation.

"You no like?" he chirped with forced cheerfulness.

The look on my face was enough to give him an answer,

"OK! Sorry, tonight this is all we have."

We were not that desperate.

After encountering such a grim place, the sight of our little van, stranded like a beached whale on that vast and empty car park, was so welcoming it seemed to us far preferable than any five star hotel. The best and only thing we could do in the circumstances was to spend the night right there. After all, I was assured that it didn't qualify as, and therefore wasn't quite as scary as *wild camping*, because there were at least a few people about, and *Montserrat* had a benign atmosphere, apart obviously from that awful *pension*. When later a huge German *Hymer* turned up on 'our' car park also to stay overnight, I could relax because of the 'safety in numbers' theory, and began to enjoy the amazing view of distant Barcelona and the Mediterranean beyond. In the darkness, a million lights began to twinkle in the vast landscape spread below us like a sequined quilt. It was another of those magical moments. From our cliff-edge perch, we soon forgot about the day's disappointments.

On the way up, we'd noticed long stretches of the roadside leading to the village and monastery were marked out for car parking. Along with this, as I've already mentioned, the car park where we were staying was not the only one. In fact ours was actually built partly suspended over the edge of the cliff; something that luckily we did not realise until the next day. It was a puzzle why they needed so many spaces. There was not much else up there apart from the Basilica and monastery, the hotel, 'pension' and hostels plus a few small shops. None of these would require so many parking places, unless the monks had a lucrative side-line in car-boot sales.

The village that night was populated for the most part by groups of baseball-hatted youngsters, whose uniforms suggested they were part of some sort of boy-scout organisation. A contingent of them appeared to be staying in a large building next to the monastery, and the happy racket emanating from it echoed round the village. Shortly before midnight, the leaders of these unruly packs, who themselves were not much older than their charges, decided to annex our car park as a playground. We guessed the thinking behind this was that the youngsters would wear themselves out, allowing their youthful commanders to get some well-earned rest themselves that night.

They were a noisy bunch, but we had no objection to this until one of the games they decided to play involved the little darlings charging up to our van and banging on the side of it. We didn't appreciate our home being used as a giant bongo drum and the sound inside our intimate haven was not pleasant. But we'd patiently put up with it a few times when without warning, Harry leapt out of the van and began shouting at them. This in itself would not have been remarkable except that he used his best '*Rab C. Nesbitt*' impression to do so.

"Ah clear aff tha' lo' o' yous!" he yelled, shaking his fist at them in the time-honoured Govan manner.

They all screamed and ran away from this maniac, and probably for the rest of their lives will be under the (almost true) impression that the British are barking mad! After this excitement, the night was thankfully incident free. Even the bells stopped, and we knew we'd made the right choice in deciding to stay beneath the protection of that lovely monastery.

It was not until we were eating our breakfast fairly early the next morning that we became aware of things stirring outside. Our tranquil and deserted surroundings, usually known as a car park, was beginning to live up to its name as it disappeared beneath an inundation of coaches and their occupants. There was complete uproar all around us as a fleet of these turned up, each one disgorging its merry Sunday horde of young and old, male and female. Having had several acres of tarmac practically to ourselves the previous night, we of course chose to park right in the middle of several coach spaces.

"I think we'd better move."

"I'm not too sure if we can now," I said looking out of the van window.

We were surrounded, but at least we now knew why they needed all of those parking spaces, even if we didn't know the reason why this place had all of a sudden become a magnet for the world and his wife. Finding an answer to this question was not as urgent as our need to bolt everything down and extricate ourselves from the chaos.

I watched as Harry climbed out of the van and began to talk to some of the drivers. Luckily they proved to be more cheerful than many of their Isle of Wight counterparts, and helped us to manoeuvre our way out of what had by now become a metal and glass maze. They held back the disembarking crowds and actually moved some of their vehicles to make things easier.

Leaving Harry to find somewhere else to park, quite a task in itself considering the tidal wave of humanity engulfing the village, I followed the crowd up to the huge square next to the Basilica, arranging to meet there eventually. As I passed the tourist office, I decided to enquire what the special occasion was on that day.

"Oh, its just a usual Sunday," the young woman there informed me.

Apparently so usual that it was not even worth a mention in the guidebook. I just had to stop relying on it for useful information.

Up in the square, people were lining all four sides en masse, and the eerie, savage sound of a *Catalan* band penetrated and rose above the cacophony. The music created an electric atmosphere, and I was keen to know why such excitement was mounting. The crowd were practically hysterical when groups of costumed people of all ages entered the arena preceded by a placard denoting the town, village or church they were allied to. Even babes in arms were dressed in *espadrilles* and every manner of colourful Spanish national dress. When there was little space left, each of these groups took it in turn to dance their particular set whilst the rest of the participants clapped and bobbed up and down to the music. Occasionally, everyone joined in the dance, resulting in confusion when some of the younger members went wrong causing an inelegant pile-up on the dance floor. The best thing about all this was that it appeared to be a genuinely 'local' event, not put on specially for tourists. We seemed to be the only foreigners there, though those Germans from the *Hymer* must have been somewhere in the crowd. In a way it was lucky there was no mention of these festivities in the guidebook.

Harry returned to the square, and having achieved the almost impossible task of finding somewhere else to park, topped this by actually managing to find me amongst the crowd. By then it was mid morning, so we decided to leave the now sweltering village and take the little rack railway to find the peace and coolness which we were certain existed at the top of the mountain. How right we were. The air on that mountaintop was as fresh and clear as any we'd found in the Alps. From the summit, the views were even more breathtaking than those from our car park home of the night before, and to my horror, we could also see the void beneath the bit we'd chosen to spend the night on.

Many signposted footpaths beckoned us to follow them, but we had to resist because the estimated times and distances to various intriguingly named destinations were a little ambitious for an afternoon stroll. Besides which, we were not prepared for a hike. Instead we admired the pretty wildflowers growing in abundance and wondered at strange birds scampering in the undergrowth or soaring on the thermals above. The revels far below us were still in full swing, and through the binoculars we could see huge *papier-mâché* figures of a man and woman causing mayhem around the square. The piercing drone of those *Catalan* pipes drifted up to our vantage point like an eerie echo of more primitive times.

It was reassuring to discover that traditions and simple pleasures like those at *Montserrat* that day still existed in Spain, perpetuated by and for its own people. Rather than being some tawdry faux-traditional attraction to tempt holiday-makers from their pool-side bars, here was proof that there were still places unspoilt by tourism. Our hitchhiker had done us a favour by being "economical with the truth". I was in my usual way, quick to condemn, but if she'd been entirely honest in the first place, *Montserrat* would still be merely a photograph in a guidebook.

Note (1) Laurie Lee 'As I Walked Out One Midsummer Morning'

When in Rome…

"Is it possible to camp here? … Now?" I was trying to say, in my best Italian.

"Ees a campsite," he groaned, in his most exasperated English.

Think of a scowling *Marvin the Paranoid Android*[1] with the appearance of a gnarled 70-something man and you get the picture of the person 'greeting' would-be campers that day at the *Campeggio Roma* on the *Via Aurelia*. You could almost hear him thinking:

"Brain the size of a planet and they get me to sit in this hut all day dealing with a load of cheap-skate campers."

He'd clearly had enough of these pesky foreigners for one day, even though it was only 10.30am. Then, in an accent so thick you would have needed a particularly strong knife to cut through, he brought our 'conversation' to a halt.

"Speeka-de-Inglish." I felt even flatter than the tone of his voice.

Obviously when in power, Mussolini had closed all the charm schools. Where were all those famous Latin Lotharios when you wanted one? This was not a good introduction to Rome.

That morning on the *via Aurelia*, I'd been more than usually unsure as to what I was actually going to say. I think it was the shock and awe of arriving at a site so early in the day which prevented me from thinking straight, though I had the nagging feeling that travelling in our camper-van was so exhausting, my brain was becoming addled. The problem was this:

We were still fairly new to the game, so I wasn't sure if prospective campers arriving before noon were able to book in. Since most sites set the deadline for <u>leaving</u> at 11 or 12 a.m. there was some logic to this. Not being early risers, it was always a bit of a mad rush for us in the morning. There is so much to do before it's possible to leave. You can't dump the dirty dishes in the sink to catch up with later, throw everything else in a heap to sort out when you get back, jump in the car and set off for the day. A campervan, is your home and you just can't move the thing, until everything is ship shape (to use the wrong analogy) and then some. Even basic things such as breakfasting, washing up breakfast things, showering, dressing, tooth-brushing are impossible to achieve before the bed itself has been folded up to give yourselves a bit of space to do them in. Then in order that nothing dislodges itself or rattles during the journey, everything has to be stowed away or anchored down. So we made a list:

- Bolt doors
- Bolt drawers
- Turn off switches
- Turn on switches
- Turn off *Gaz* bottle stop cock
- Empty waste containers
- Fill water containers
- Unplug electricity cable from mains
- Coil electricity cable
- Stow electricity cable
- Drain hoses
- Coil hoses
- Stow hoses
- Tie back curtains
- Secure fridge door
- Weigh down grill pan *(really annoying when it rattles)*

- Secure oven door *(also causes an annoying rattle)*
- Strap down loo *(messy if you forget and take a winding road)*
- Place peg on loo roll centre *(serves to stop the whole thing looking like the Andrex puppy has tried running off with it)*
- Roll up awning

I'm sure there are a few I've missed, though unfortunately, we often forgot to look at the list anyway. Maybe this should have been on another to do list. We seldom got 200 yards up the road before the clonking started somewhere on board and we had to stop and sort it out. Once even, we tried driving away with the awning still erected. That really **was** embarrassing. Eventually when this marathon of organisation had been accomplished, we then needed to pore over maps to decide our route for the day. In short, quitting a campsite felt like launching an expedition to the back of beyond.

It's easy to see why we'd never before managed the feat of arriving at a site before midday, and it only happened on this occasion because we'd stayed the previous night just a short distance along the coast to the north of Rome on a site innocently calling itself *The Camping Queen*. Of course anyone with a bit of common sense would tell you that it is only the actual number of nights you stay which counts, but even my normally logical Other Half had not really sussed this one out. Still, we'd found that people running campsites were only too willing to make you feel welcome, and any attempt at their language, no matter how pathetic, was always appreciated. With this in mind I was certain that there would be no problem in trying to establish whether we could book in straight away. How wrong can you be?

Why was it that whenever I presented myself at a campsite reception, in front of me were always a Dutch couple with a caravan? That day was no exception. Eventually, their business with *Marvin* finished, the *Nederlanders* turned away from the hut to leave, and trying to be friendly, I smiled and said *sotto voce* and with what I thought was witty sarcasm,

"He's a cheerful chap!"

I should of course have realised that being from Holland meant that though charming and speaking impeccable English, they did not share my British sense of humour. My remark was greeted with blank stares and straight faces. They probably thought *Marvin's* personality was quite normal. Still, I was determined not to be down-hearted, and once *mine host* had left me in no doubt as to my considerable inadequacies in the language department, we found a place to pitch up and left for the delights of the Eternal City.

The confidence gained by our trouble-free use of the Spanish Metro the previous year turned out to be a double-edged sword in Rome. It's underground system may be quite modern compared to parts of the tube in London, but give me the Northern Line any day. The Roman metro consists of two lines, 'A' and 'B', which cross at only one point, the *Stazione Termini*. Unfortunately, *Termini* is also the mainline railway station for the city, with the resulting chaos of huge crowds of commuters and tourists resembling a swarm of termites as they converge at one point from many directions. *Termini* as a result, is fertile ground for crime.

Living in as comparatively safe a place as the Isle of Wight could make one a little complacent about crime, and street crime in particular. Although robberies and muggings do happen and even murder has been known, it must be like utopia to most city dwellers. We were both brought up in and around London so are not so naïve as to expect to saunter around foreign parts with the same attitude we would have on the Island. I'd especially bought myself a new and more secure handbag for that first trip to Italy. Since I was under no illusion that this bag would make me pickpocket or bag-snatcher proof, I also made sure that I jammed it to my side whilst out and about. But rogues on the Roman Metro certainly possessed outstanding skills.

Though there were not huge numbers of people waiting on the platform that morning, when the train arrived there was a bit of a surge to get on. In true British fashion, we politely stood aside to allow passengers to get out of the train, and when it seemed that all who wanted to had disembarked, we moved forward to get on ourselves. At this moment a group of eccentrically dressed elderly women rushed out of the carriage door like a herd of marauding football fans, shoving me aside and knocking me off balance. In my usual way I was a bit put out by this, but assumed that they had at the last minute realised they were at their stop. During the kafuffle, my arm was shoved away from my side where it was clamping my handbag, which in turn swung loose behind my back. I thought nothing more about this until we arrived at our aimed for station, when I realised my bag was open and began to rummage in it.

"Oh my God! My purse has gone!"

"It must be there," Harry replied, "you carry so much junk round, how can you tell?"

I rummaged again, but it wasn't there. Was it possible that in that split second, someone had put their hand inside and helped themselves? My suspicions lay with a smartly dressed woman I'd noticed eyeing us on the platform when we first arrived. We were used to people staring at us like we were relatives of *Mr Spock*, but I had the feeling that time I looked more like an easy 'dip' than *Leonard Nimmoy's* sister. The only consolation was that my credit cards, camera and both our passports were still there but in a separate compartment. Even though my purse contained little actual cash, the gutting thing was that for once I had the foresight to buy Italian stamps for my postcards as soon as the opportunity presented itself once in Italy. Now I would still have my usual frustrating search for a post office and these precious examples of my abnormal efficiency were in the hands of some low-life.

I was feeling violated and stupid for letting it happen to *me*. Harry was wearing a sort of *"well-you-should-have-taken-more-care-of-your-bag"* look on his face and by the time we got to street level and the booking hall of the station I was in a rage. Indignation propelled me to the ticket office where the unfortunate girl there became the object of my displeasure.

"I've been robbed! I know you can't do anything about it, but YOU SHOULD KNOW!"

Luckily for me she spoke English and realised that I was not some escaped madwoman, and was probably quite used to incoherent, angry foreigners. She called over a young man in uniform who was adorning the station foyer, his red beret tilted at a rakish angle, and so immaculate of appearance that he could have been straight out of *Cine Città* Central Casting. Presumably he was some sort of transport policeman.

"Eet 'appen all ze time 'ere," he said, charmingly shrugging his muscle-bound shoulders.

No mystery then as to why these robberies were so common if the perpetrators knew that the law preferred to stand up there looking like a young Marlon Brando. Why should Marlon risk creasing his *Chinos* or scuffing those shiny boots while patrolling the platforms amongst the plebs below? It seemed impossible to take matters any further, so we gave up trying and allowed the star to carry on radiating glamour in the booking hall.

The next day found us again on the platform at Termini. This time I was without my handbag, preferring to hang on to what I had left in the way of possessions by carrying everything I needed for the day in a small zipped holdall with the strap diagonally across my shoulder in the manner of the locals (I had belatedly noticed this the day before). Any prospective thieves would have to take me as well as my bag. As we waited for the train, a young woman struggling with a large case on wheels stood next to us, and on her back she was carrying one of those small handbag-sized rucksacks that were just becoming fashionable at the time. Because of our unhappy experience at that place and the obvious fact that her rucksack was unzipped at the top, Harry, ever the helpful citizen, took it on himself to warn her that this could be a temptation to the deviants prowling the underground system.

"Excuse me, but did you know your bag is open?" he said, "My wife was robbed on this platform yesterday!"

"Oh my god!" she exclaimed with a perfect American accent. "I'm from Rome, so I should have been more careful!"

"Well you probably didn't need us to warn you then!" I said.

Still, she seemed to appreciate our concern, and when the train arrived, Harry offered to carry her suitcase onto it. This wasn't just being courteous. The huge gap between train and platform required a leap rather than a mere step to get across it.

There was the usual undignified scramble of people trying simultaneously to get off and on as only can be achieved by societies which haven't quite got to grips with the concept of queuing. We waited for the mayhem to calm, but by then it was standing room only inside the carriage. I gripped my bag to my chest as though my life depended on it. Everyone stood packed closely together like tied bunches of asparagus ready for steaming. As the train idled on the platform, a smartly dressed man tapped on our new acquaintance's shoulder, pointed to her rucksack and said something in Italian. She swiftly took it off of her back and began to delve into it frantically.

"What's the matter?" I asked.

"Someone had their hand in my bag, and my wallet has gone!"

As she said this, Harry reached down and started patting the pockets on the sides of his 'combat' style trousers. I looked at him with a sense of foreboding.

"Oh no ... what's happened?"

"You're not going to believe this," he said with an ironic smile on his face. "My money's gone too!"

This really was too much. Those thieves were certainly slick. By observing us buying tickets earlier, they must have known where the money was kept. No doubt this method is an easy and reliable way to locate the wallet of an unsuspecting tourist: just see where they put it back after a transaction and it's a gift! With his usual good sense, and in an effort to minimise any loss in the event of this kind of thing happening, Harry did not carry round his actual wallet, but kept a small amount of cash and a credit card in one of those small plastic wallets which railcards etc. are supplied in. The rest of the cards and cash were left well hidden in a specially devised cubby hole in the van. Even so, it was extremely maddening to have been caught twice, and in the same place. Then the awful thought occurred to me. I turned to Harry and said in a low voice,

"I hope she doesn't think we had anything to do with losing her wallet!"

I was so embarrassed.

Although we had brought more than one card away with us, the one stolen was, of course the only card we knew the PIN for. When we next tried to get cash out of a bank, we realised how much hassle this had created. But that's another story…[2]

I was looking forward to paying when we left *Camping Roma* the following day. Not because I wanted to be parted with our money for once *voluntarily*, but because I was preparing for a showdown with my old pal *Marvin* at the reception. He'd annoyed me so much on our arrival that I felt quite justified in making him the target of my simmering dissatisfaction with his City. I looked up all the right words in my Italian/English dictionary. Words such as 'thief', 'scum', 'crooks', that kind of thing.

Inevitably I didn't have the chance to give my rehearsed diatribe, because it was not the intended object of my displeasure working in reception that morning. When I arrived at the window, instead of Marvin, there was a young woman. She was chatting on the phone, but as soon as he saw me, she ended the call.

"Oh I'm so sorry for keeping you waiting!"

Considering I'd only been there a nano-second before she put the phone down, I was taken aback by such politeness. I was hoping I could pay for the site by credit card as we had little cash left, and explained about having a card and cash stolen over the previous two days.

"Oh dear, so many people are robbed on the buses now," she sympathised.

"But we were robbed on the Metro!" I replied.

By not being victims on both means of Roman transport it appeared we'd got off lightly. She apologised profusely for our unhappy experience of her city and seemed to feel personally responsible for our bad luck. In a way I was pleased not to have had another close encounter with my old adversary, for at least we left the site and the city with a better impression than we had on arrival.

The small dissatisfactions with our welcome in Rome were as nothing compared to the experience of a young English couple we met during a later Italian trip. We were taking in the evening air on a lovely campsite just outside Bologna, and noticed a young couple making their way bent almost double, along the roadway towards us. Like donkeys in a third world country, they were piled to what looked like nearing the final straw. Each carried a huge rucksack from which dangled all manner of camping and cooking paraphernalia. They off-loaded and set up their tent on a pitch diagonally opposite to ours, and we admired the tenacity of youth at carting all that stuff round with them. A short while later, the young lad approached us.

"Hi, we've just got here" he said unnecessarily, pointing to the tent. "Hope you don't mind me asking but I don't suppose you've got any vegetables to spare we could buy off of you? We haven't had a chance to shop and the one on site is shut."

We were pleased to be able to help, and for no charge sorted out a courgette, onion, carrots and tomatoes, along with a carton of wine. He was really grateful, and began to tell us what had happened to them.

"We're on our gap year – just finished our A levels. We DID have a camper van but it was stolen."

He continued as we sat listening in disbelief.

"Yeah. We were staying on the ___(3) site in Rome. Went to do a bit of sight-seeing and when we got back it was gone. No-one knew anything or saw anything. Just disappeared with all our stuff in."

We'd heard about this notorious site before from fellow travellers – the rumour machine was an interesting part of campsite life. The word was that the Mafia controlled it, but whether this was true or not, I couldn't say. The place apparently was rife with petty and not so petty theft. Of course most of the young back-packers and Australian *'Bus-About'*(4) travellers etc. staying there only found this out after they had become victims. We too were ignorant of this when we arrived in Rome during our first time in Italy, but luckily intended to stay at *Campeggio Roma* anyway.

" We were left with what we were wearing, though luckily we had our passports and cards with us," he went on.

"Well I suppose you could say you were lucky you didn't get those lifted while you were sight-seeing!" I piped in, trying to look on the bright side.

If they had been panicked by their loss, they certainly weren't showing it. Now if this had been me, you wouldn't have seen me for dust. I'd have been on the first train/plane home, damning the whole country to hell and vowing never to return. Fortunately, everyone isn't like me, and our young neighbours decided to buy a tent and all that goes with it to continue their tour regardless. Hence the saucepans hanging from the rucksacks.

The next day we were hoping to wish them *bon voyage* before they left, but by the time we returned from our morning in Bologna, they'd crammed everything back into those economy-sized backpacks, placed the half-consumed wine carton on our van doorstep and departed for pastures new. I would like to say that I had such determination at their age, but if I did, I would be lying.

Notes
(1) Douglas Adams, Hitch-Hikers Guide to the Galaxy
(2) See chapter 17 – Money, Money, Money
(3) For the purposes of wanting not to get a contract on me, this site will remain unnamed.
(4) A means of back-packing where bus travellers are dropped off at various places around Europe and picked up at pre-arranged times. We met many of these intrepid travellers and not all of them were that young!

Rome – Shouting in the Sistine

The scene:
Rome: A gateway into the Vatican grounds watched over by a Swiss Guard already dressed for Panto season.

The action:
In full view of the rubber-necked Barbarians at the gate, *Julie Andrews*, in the guise of Sister Maria approaches the sentry box where she produces a letter from her shoulder bag and presents it to our friend in fancy dress. He in turn opens and peruses the missive. Lifting the telephone in the sentry box, he speaks to someone and it's not long before one of the *Corleoni* family arrives, brandishing his radio and sporting *Raybans*. His black suit may well conceal a gun. Unfortunately for him, he is played by *Dan Aykroyd* with a beer-gut, so not at all menacing even if he thought he was.

Dan reads the letter, lifts the 'phone, speaks to someone, then hands the receiver to Sister Julie, who by now looks a darker shade of pink in the face than she did before, obviously uncomfortable at this all going on in front of a large audience. After a protracted conversation with the unseen at the other end of the line, eventually she replaces the receiver. The letter is folded and returned to her. She laughs self-consciously and disappears into the rabble, her head held high and smiling radiantly. To be turned away so unceremoniously in front of so many people was not much fun. But I think the crowd were on her side.

We wondered why would they not let her in.

"Your Eminence, we 'ave a young nun 'ere wiz a letter of recommendation,"

"Ees-a she-a good-a lookin'?"

"Well in a Julie Andrews a-way, sire,"

"Put 'er on,"

"The hills are alive, with the sound of music!" Julie warbles.

"Mi dispiace, cara. Zee auditions, zey were yesterday!"

I frequently got the feeling that we were the only people with a sense of humour in Rome. Like most tourists, a visit to the Vatican and its museums was high on our list of priorities. We'd tried to visit the museum unsuccessfully on our first day, along with a large number of other people from around the world, and America in particular. With nothing or no-one at the supposed entrance to suggest why it was closed, or whether in fact that it was the entrance at all, the crowd gathered around its shiny facade at a loss for what to do next. Harry, not one to stand around unnecessarily, took the initiative and asked a waiting taxi driver if he knew the reason for the closure.

"Ees a holy day," he said, "you want leeft somewhere else?"

"Well *we* don't thanks, but stick around as there may be one or two who *will* want one when I tell them what's going on."

We of course had the excuse of not being Catholic, but some of our fellow would-be visitors shrieked with embarrassment when he told them.

"Oh no, I'm Catholic and should have known!" was the gist of these shrieks.

At least we could return the next day, but for some who had travelled from far-flung places outside Europe, this was the only day they had in Rome. It seemed rather remiss not to post even a small notice on that very large door.

Returning the following day, we joined the queue, and again this was made up with a large and exuberant contingency of American youth. Disappointingly for many of the female members of this group, they were still unable to enter. It seemed that the wearing of strappy tops was a big *no-no* in the Vatican grounds. To show a bare shoulder was the height of indecency, though considering that the ceiling of the Sistine Chapel contains acres of naked flesh, both male and female[1], the rule seemed rather incongruous. This only served to confirm my theory that any rule derived by man from religious doctrine rarely makes sense when examined too closely.

We were more-by-luck-than-judgement appropriately attired for a visit to the hallowed halls, and leaving the embarrassed young women to scrabble for scarves and jumpers to drape over their offending appendages, we were allowed to enter. As we wandered through the corridors lined by a multitude of golden trinkets, religious sculptures and paintings, it was refreshing to come across the *Stanza della Segnatura* containing Raphael's frescos. His *School of Athens* made a nice change from some saint or other gazing skywards with a look of ecstasy on his or her face. The sight of all those ancient philosophers and mathematicians in deep discussion and thought was a breath of fresh air amongst a mawkish quagmire. I looked out for my favourite figure: the 'plagerist' looking over *Pythagoras'* shoulder. What a brilliant observation of human nature by that artist who, unusually, was so well-beloved during his lifetime.

But all roads in the Vatican lead not to *Rome* (since we are already there) but to the Sistine Chapel. Inevitably there is a bottle-neck before entering the chapel itself. Whilst in this bottle-neck, you are treated to an announcement. This announcement is helpfully in a number of languages, and tells you that as the chapel is a place of worship, visitors should keep silent during their visit. This seemed fair enough since many tourists fail to respect the sanctity of religious buildings and merely treat them as somewhere else they can tick off of their list. Before we entered the chapel, the introduction to the German part of the proclamation amused us no end because it sounded more like something from the *Great Escape*:

"*Achtung, Achtung…*"

When we realised that the announcements to maintain silence continued to be broadcast actually **inside** the chapel, it was difficult to keep a straight face. If they thought the aura of sanctity would be enhanced by all that shouting, they were very much mistaken.

The presence throughout the Vatican of those dark-suited and sunglass-wearing security guards, did not add to any feeling of spirituality either. Those waiting at the entrance doors of the basilica of Saint Peter, ready to pounce on the 'under-dressed' visitor, seemed really menacing with their 'walkie-talkies' constantly crackling. No President of the United States could have been better protected from an assassin than those sacred walls were from the dangerous sight of bare shoulders. The first time we visited, I was wearing a T-shirt, but I was lucky to get away with my sleeveless (not strappy) dress the following day. The guard was on the point of challenge when someone in shorts caught his eye, and he made a bee-line for them instead. Bare knees it seemed, trumped tops of arms.

It was away from the Vatican that a small kindness shown to us would go some way to restoring our good opinion of the Catholic Church. We'd been trying to find a cut through into the Botanic Gardens above *Trastevere*. As usual, our map seemed to be the work of a Graphic Designer rather than a Cartographer in that did not bear any resemblance to the actual layout of Rome but was lovely to peruse. We found ourselves walking for some distance along on a road which began to look a bit like the sort of place they warn you not to wander into, it being adorned with litter, graffiti and clusters of shifty looking youths. On the opposite side of the road to us was a high brick wall that stretched as far as the eye could see.

"The gardens must be behind that wall," Harry was convinced his map-reading skills had not deserted him completely.

"Well if they are, I can't see any way in."

It felt like that frustrating scene in *Alice In Wonderland* where she keeps trying to get into the lovely garden she knows is beyond a gateway and is either too big or too small. In our case though, there was no obvious entrance into the place even if we were the right size. Just as I was beginning to get that all too familiar panicky feeling, we noticed a young man unlocking a previously invisible door in the wall, and seizing our chance, we found a gap in the traffic and crossed over.

"Please can you help? We're trying to find the Botanic Gardens. Are they behind this wall?"

Fortunately he spoke a little English.

"Sorry, this is the Seminary!"

Our faces dropped.

"You can go through to get to gardens. I take you."

With the busy road running out of pavement and those youths, to my mind, looking more menacing by the minute, this young priest was our saviour. He ushered us through the door and like Alice, we found ourselves in another world. Tennis courts, lush lawns, mature trees and beautiful flowerbeds formed this peaceful haven amidst the traffic-clogged streets of Rome. There was the atmosphere of any International College except it was only young men playing tennis, kicking footballs, jogging or just relaxing and reading. Any moment I feared I might be rumbled as an illegal female presence in this male-only environment, but our companion was quite relaxed to be walking along with us both in tow. I attempted conversation to give the impression I was meant to be there, in case anyone was watching. It turned out that his first language was French, a fact that oiled the conversation somewhat.

"I hope you won't mind me asking, but are you a student here?"

"Oh yes. I'm from *Bequino Faso*. It is a small country in Africa. I have another two years before I qualify, and then I want to go back and try to make a difference."

I was very interested to know if they still used the Latin language in their studies because I'd learnt it at school.

UNEASY RIDER

"Oh no!" he laughed, "We don't need to know Latin any more!"

I was disappointed. If Latin was no longer required as part of the training for the priesthood it did seem a shame, and with the Catholic Church abandoning Latin, who else would keep it going? But this was not the right time for my soapbox to come out.

We enjoyed chatting our way through those lovely grounds with such pleasant company when all too soon it was time to shake hands with our companion, wish each other *"Bon Chance!"* and take our leave. I like to imagine that the parishioners of this charming man are now benefiting from him "making a difference" to their lives.

Such chance encounters enriched our travels. Asking directions from a passing local was invariably greeted with a smile and a willingness to help that made me feel guilty for cursing their country/town/government for the inaccurate maps/lack of legible road signs/diversions etc. that had got us lost in the first place. The flexibility of not being part of a 'package' and making your own way around can have its problems, but even in Rome there can be rewards.

Notes (1) In fact Michelangelo used male models for his naked female figures in the fresco, adding bits where necessary.

Money, Money, Money
Down but not out in Casino (amongst other places)

I stood in front of the final till at the remaining untried bank in Casino.

"I have no money … robbed in Rome …nothing to eat or drink…"

The eating and drinking gambit was rather stretching the truth, but it had been a while since breakfast …

The theft in Rome of our only pin-number-known cash card[1] made me realise how easy it could be to become destitute in a foreign country. We take for granted the ease of access to our money at home, and the need to physically carry cash around in large amounts is a thing of the past unless you're a builder or slot-machine-arcade proprietor. There's even less inclination to be in possession of too much currency whilst travelling, so the sight of a hole in the wall cash machine is often as welcome as – well a hole-in-the-wall cash machine actually. Inexplicably quirky opening times of banks in foreign lands make the loss of your *flexible friend* a catastrophe beyond reason. At least beyond my reason anyway.

Italy at one time was a difficult place to find anywhere to accept credit cards for payment, presumably because of its dodgy history of mafia fraud, but by and large we'd found it much more accommodating during latter visits to that country. However, on one occasion a few years before the Euro came into being, lack of cash almost left us stranded in the Italian Alps when we had crossed from France by car for a day trip. Relying on filling up with petrol bought by our *flexible friend* once there, the chance of finding a service station which would accept it was about as good as Great Britain winning more than two medals at the Winter Olympics (well, this *was* the Alps). The only reason we were in the end able to make the return journey was that this wasn't a weekend or one of the multitude of Holy feast days. Days that had left us without bread and milk in many places.

Even so, we were lucky that there actually was a bank in the ski resort we'd managed to reach. Being mid September and the limbo season between summer sun and winter snow, there was nothing to do because nowhere was bothering to open for a few late stragglers. With no cash machine outside the bank, we had to hang around aimlessly for opening time after the four hour 'lunch' break - we daren't try to find anywhere else further on.

One of the reasons for making this journey was in the hope of finding better weather on the Italian side of the Alps, but to add to our frustration, it was pouring with rain there too and we did not even have a view of the mountains by way of compensation. We sat dejectedly in the chilly confines of the car.

"We could go for a walk," suggested my Other Half.

"I didn't bother to put the boots in – for some reason we expected it to be sunny here remember!"

So we sat watching the 1970s concrete buildings blacken gloomily in the drizzle. No doubt in winter the snows cover up a multitude of ugly architectural sins, endowing these eyesores with a magical air. The byways of the town probably resemble a carnival in Rio as they buzz with the camaraderie of winter sports and the brightly garbed ski set. All this was difficult to imagine that drab afternoon.

"Wouldn't it be nice to be curled up at home in front of the telly?" I said as the fog closed in.

When the bank eventually opened and we were able to exchange our Francs, hope was restored somewhat by not only having the wherewithal to buy petrol but also to get a drink in the only place that seemed to be open: an English Pub. I've often bemoaned the existence of such places abroad, but the gaudy fluorescent sign announcing *The Red Lion* and the Liverpool accent of its chatty young landlord were more welcome at that moment than a lottery win. British-style loos also came as a pleasant surprise. One can always rely on those good old traditions even in Italy.

If that day in the Italian Alps had been an awkward one monetarily speaking, a few years later, matters would prove a little more difficult to resolve at *Casino*. We'd eeked out enough cash to stay on the *Campeggio Zeus* at *Pompeii,* and later even managed to get up to the crater of Vesuvius with the use of British currency[2], but by the time we were heading northwards towards Assisi and Venice, I was beginning to feel that our situation was becoming desperate. For once, we'd arrived in the first large town on our route, namely Casino, at a time when the banks were actually open. There were cash machines a-plenty outside these establishments, but they were of no use to us because although we still had several other cards in our possession, it of course was the one stolen in Rome which Harry knew the *pin* for. The only way to get at any money was over a till. It would be easy enough we thought, but with no empty parking spaces in the *piazza*, it was up to me to *do the business* while Harry waited in the van.

Things are never quite as simple as they should be. Like a spectator at Wimbledon, he sat and watched me cross that square from side to side as I was sent in turn by each of these so-called banks to annoy the competition across the way.

"Scusi, signora, but you go to uzzer bank in piazza. Arriverderci!" became a familiar phrase, but at least I got the brush-off in English.

It seemed too much to expect a bank to produce any actual money. My numerous dashes across Centre Court meant that the big lunchtime closedown was now imminent, but just trying to gain entry into the final place was proving extremely difficult. I spent several minutes desperately exploring the frontage of the building before realising that the narrow, curved and blackened glass on the corner of the premises was actually the entrance. It would have looked more at home on the set of a Star Wars film rather than a Neo-Classical facade. Somehow I managed to get inside what turned out to be an air-lock, but in the process felt that any customer with a degree of claustrophobia worse than mine would be at a distinct disadvantage. And someone confined to wheelchair was obviously *persona non grata*. But if merely getting inside had been a trial, this was just the initiation.

I joined the queue for the first till. The person at the head of it was unfortunately sorting out the finances of a debt-ridden third world country, so by the time I reached the desk I was already a bit fed up.

"Per favore," I tried.

"Si signora?" the bored but elegant clerk acknowledged my existence at last.

I brandished my cash card and passport.

"Per favore. Vorrei …"

But that was as far as I got.

He pointed a manicured finger towards the door.

"You must…" he began.

I'd given up on the Italian by then.

"Sorry, but I've already tried the other banks! I only need…"

" Ze machine outside. You must use eet,"

"I have no pin, the card for it was stolen!" I tried to explain.

"You must go…"

"Here we go again," I thought.

"… to ze next till."

Well that was better than being thrown out, I supposed.

I stood behind yet another Third World Finance Minister. The whole previous episode was repeated, my teeth being so gritted by now that I could hardly open my mouth. With feigned calm I again explained I had no *pin* number, *the card with the pin having been stolen in their lovely capital city.* This was Groundhog Day.

I was running out of queues to line up in and found myself at the final till at the end of the beautifully polished mahogany counter. And also the end of my rather shabby tether. Other customers in the bank were staring by now and it all became too much.

"I wouldn't have all this trouble in England, people are more trusting there!"

Well it seemed like a good idea to say it at the time.

Choking back the tears, I was treated to the same cop-out suggestion for solving my cash problem.

"My card with the pin was stolen," the veneer of politeness so thin now it was see-through.

My British stiff upper lip trembled, my head throbbed and the words became incoherent as I choked back the tears. Unintentionally, I found myself playing the sympathy card with the food and drink ploy and luckily this seemed to do the trick. Probably not wanting to miss out on any of his lunch break by dealing with an unconscious tourist, the clerk asked to see my passport. I only wanted the equivalent of about £100 in cash, and it stood to reason that if I were a *bona fide* crook, I would be trying to get the maximum amount of £250 out of them.

At last the begrudging wheels of Italian bureaucracy began to grind, and a colleague was summoned from the depths of a rear office. They both retreated behind the glass window and went into a lengthy discussion, every so often glancing up at this mad-woman who had the cheek to ask for money *from a bank*. Phone calls were made, photo-copies of my passport taken and I lost count of the number of things I had to put my signature to – as everything was in Italian I just hoped that I was not signing up to any type of Faustian deal.

By this time, Harry was wondering why I was, as usual, taking so long to do such a simple thing. I could almost hear him thinking,

"What on earth is she doing in there – I should have gone myself!"

If only he had.

Leaving the van to the risk of being towed-away, he managed to get through the air-lock with a great deal more ease than I had, and discovered me in a heap at the far counter. Of course by then, it was all being sorted out, so he did not have to play Knight In Shining Armour for once. They wouldn't have pushed Sir Galahad from one till to the next for such a piffling amount of money. Like motor mechanics and builders anywhere, they assumed that they could treat a lone woman with dismissive contempt. Maybe if I'd been a tall blonde twenty year old, I would have had a bit more co-operation, but this type of transformation being beyond my control, I decided that I was having nothing more to do with the Italian banking system.

Occasionally though, being short of the *readies* resulted in, shall I say, a more interesting day than had been planned.

Whilst touring the *Auvergne* region of France, I made the silly mistake of using euros in the supermarket instead of the card, and having to pay cash for our stay at the little municipal site at *Volvic*, left us brassic once again. We intended the next morning to drive up the *Puy de Dôme*. My guidebook stated that it was possible to drive up the *Puy*, but of course this was not the case. We'd have to leave the van at the base rather than take it to the summit, and as we looked at the board in the car park displaying the fares, we realised a return trip was beyond our present means. From past experience, we weren't entirely surprised they didn't accept payment by card.

The area is so beautiful with its extinct volcanoes and shining craters. It would have been a pity to turn away without visiting the highest point. We decided to take the bus up and walk down

– we needed the exercise anyway – so logically the cost would be halved.

"S'il vous plait, two one-way tickets, err, *duex aller*?" I asked the young girl at the ticket office.

"Je suis desolée, Madame. Eese only aller-retour, return treep."

To our minds, it seemed unlikely that no-one before had wanted to walk down from the *Puy*. The existence of large boards displaying maps of the myriad footpaths in the area seemed to give the impression this was a walker's paradise.

We went back to the van and feeling like a pair of tramps trying to scrape enough money together to buy a cup of tea, searched every nook and its accompanying cranny for coins that might have been hiding in them. But there was still not quite enough to pay the advertised fare for two *aller-retours* and I began to resign myself to staying in the foothills. Unless of course Harry could come up with a cunning plan…

We'd noticed many *parapentistes* making their way to the ticket office, and several four-wheeled drive trucks with the logos of local hang gliding schools were seen trundling back and forth with the gear on board for these otherwise sane looking people to use. Before I knew what was happening, Harry was marching boldly up to the ticket office window.

"Stick with me," he said.

"Deux *parapentistes* tickets, s'il vous plait."

Parapentistes, after all, only needed to bus it upwards.

"I hope no-one challenges me for wearing sandals and cropped trousers to fling myself off a volcano - even if it **is** extinct."

I'd have liked to at least change into trainers if we were going to walk down, but with the bus about to leave I had no option but to follow my Other Half onto it. No-one questioned us though. After all, we only intended to go one way so what was the difference if we chose to descend from the *Puy de Dôme* in a more conventional fashion?

The road to the top in the comfortable, air-conditioned bus was long, steep and winding, but we still felt sure that the walk down would be well within our abilities. Once at the summit, the Ancient Roman 'Temple of Mercury' was a disappointing pile of rubble surrounded by a very unattractive chain-link fence, but the 360 degree view lived up to all expectations. It is said that one quarter of the area of France can be seen from here. Spectacular only just about covers it.

Before embarking on our way back down to base camp, rather than set out randomly on any old path, we consulted the young lady at the tourist desk in the visitor centre.

"Zis path is ok," she assured us, pointing to a squiggly line on a map.

"Is it an easy walk?" I asked, pointing to my sandals.

"Well of course!"

"Have you walked this one?"

"Non, but I know zat eet is eezy. Many people do ziss,"

"And how long will it take us?" Unfortunately for her I was full of questions.

"Oh, only une heure, hour and half maybe."

Sounded good. An easy hour and a half's walk was just what we wanted. **And** all downhill!

She pointed out where we should pick up this path, we thanked her and set off.

The footpath started well enough. A bit steep, but nothing we couldn't handle. Before long though, our gentle stroll turned into more of a manic slide, the ground having turned into the crumbling surface of the moon. In my sandals, there seemed a good chance that I would finish the holiday with a couple of limbs in plaster, but other appropriately shod walkers were also having difficulties. As I crawled my way down backwards on all-fours, it was refreshing to hear the shrieks of a lady walker behind us whose footwear would not have looked out of place on Everest.

No matter which country you are in, unknown footpaths, despite promising beginnings, in our experience tend to fizzle out. This one was no exception. There'd obviously been a sort of larva landslide recently, and treacherously sharp shale and pumice at one point obliterated the path completely. We were left clueless as to which direction to follow. The shrieking lady and her male companion had caught up with us by then. We'd been keeping them in view illogically thinking that as French nationals, they would be certain to know the right way. Well they may have if they hadn't come from Paris and despite carrying a rather impressive *Michelin* map of the area, they were as clueless as us. We all pored over the map for a while, but soon these two decided they would attempt to reach one of the other craters rather than try for the car park. It seemed the easier option.

As they disappeared along a track going in an upwards direction, I had the feeling that we would be wandering round the *Auvergne* for ever and began singing, *"I was lost in France"*, which cheered us up no end. So we plodded on, with me getting quieter the more worried, footsore and fed up I became. Harry in his usual logical and optimistic way tried to reassure me that since we were still heading downwards, we must eventually end up in the right place. Luckily it was not long before hope was revived by being almost run down by some youths tearing along wildly on mountain bikes. Assuming that they must be heading in the right direction, we managed to follow their tracks until the signs of lowland civilisation began to appear in the form of families out for a casual stroll and people exercising their dogs. None of them looked like they could have come very far, since there were both tiny infants in buggies and rather fat couples who looked as if they should have tried walking more often. They certainly would not have wandered any distance from the car park.

At last, we were back at the *parking*, and as I looked up at the beautiful and aloof *Puy* soaring high above us, I did feel a sense of achievement.

"I think people giving out advice in these tourist offices should try things out themselves before passing on misleading information to us punters," I moaned as I soaked my feet in a bucket.

My sandals were ruined and it took a long time for those lacerated feet to recover. However, it taught me a lesson not to rely on paying for anything by card again.

So if you ever see one of those mineral water ads on TV, spare a thought for that Parisian couple who may still be wandering round the Auvergne in search of a car park.

Notes
(1) See "When In Rome"
(2) See "...we got a problem..."

Pompeii
Cave Canem!
(Beware of the Dog!)

While roaming the streets of modern Pompeii looking for a likely *fruta* shop we realised we were being stalked. Our stalker was extremely thin and scruffy, possibly even a bit mangy. He also had four spindly legs and a waggy tail.

Like many before me, I'd felt drawn to visit the ill-fated town of ancient Pompeii ever since learning about it in Junior School. The images of those petrified people 'frozen' in time both fascinated and horrified, but however tragic those figures seemed, as a child it was the pathetic shape of a curled-up dog turned to stone that left a lasting impression. Children are natural animal-lovers, usually having more sympathy with the suffering of dumb creatures than fellow human beings, and the image of the dog remained with me for many years. During our visit to Pompeii the sight of his numerous ancestors prowling the streets or laying curled up in a similar manner was a sad and chilling link to the past.

The day we arrived in modern-day Pompeii, there had apparently been a victory by the neighbouring 'Serie A' *Napoli* football team. Jubilant supporters, evidently the whole population of the town, were celebrating by recklessly whizzing up and down on their Lambretta's, blasting horns and at the same time performing amazing balancing acts by brandishing the team flag which was almost half the size of a football pitch. The celebrations went on well into the night. I guess they do those things in Italy. And I guess they did such things in the first century AD when the local gladiators beat the Barbarian team from up north.

We'd decided to take the minor road south from Rome to get there, rather than the motorway, and once reaching the outskirts of Pompeii, our route took us through surprisingly green market gardens and pleasant suburbs. As usual, our first aim was to find a campsite, and for once this proved extremely easy, despite the complete absence of any being indicated in our Camping Club International book.

"I'm giving up on that CCI book," I declared, "It's only interested in telling you that there's a Sea-Life Centre nearby. And the amount they take off the site fee for using their card is pathetic."

Who needed it anyway when along the road which led to the ruins, there were several sites, all grandly bearing classically inspired names derived from ancient Roman and Greek mythology. *Spartacus* was passed by in favour of *Zeus* who after all was the main man, although our decision may also have been influenced by the discovery that the entrance to the ancient site was just a few steps away In fact so close were the excavations, we had the feeling that the ground beneath us in all probability concealed parts of the town yet to be unearthed.

That evening we took a walk along the road which ran parallel with the perimeter fence of the ruins, and were surprised to see that relatively recently, houses had been built right alongside it. Pretty gardens growing a riot of flowers and vegetables along with lush grape-vines and small orchards thrived in the rich volcanic soil. It was during this walk we discovered the astonishingly close presence of the motorway. Crossing the railway that runs near to the ancient site and then proceeds onto and around the base of the Vesuvius, there it was.

"Well I hadn't expected a toll booth and four lanes of high speed traffic, that's for sure,"

"What did you expect then?" Harry asked.

"Something a bit more remote." I moaned. My mind was full of those romantic Grand Tour paintings of ruins set in splendid isolation on top of a hill. It was becoming obvious that there must be few areas in the world, and in Europe especially, still enjoying this type of exclusivity.

When it came to campsites, we also hankered after isolation. Not having the herd instinct, we always aimed to get as far away from other 'campers' as possible. This wasn't always easy, but in on *Campeggio Zeus* finding our ideal spot was effortless. We couldn't understand why no-one else had chosen to set up on this area, but then we always seemed to be at odds with the majority. At 7 o'clock the next morning though, all was made clear. Our remote position did not seem quite so ideal when we were disturbed from our slumbers by pneumatic drills digging up the roadway crossing that part of the site. This, along with the sound of concrete mixers and the smell of tarmac, accompanied our unplanned early breakfast that day. Not for the first time during our travels, we packed everything up and moved, in an attempt to get as far away from all the commotion as possible. This was not altogether such an unfortunate thing to have happened, since our new position next to a large German motor caravan resulted in several pleasant, though totally confusing, conversations with the very nice lady occupant who spoke even less English than I did German.

Being right on the doorstep, so to speak, we were among the first to visit the ruins that day, and experienced that rare and glorious feeling of having the place almost to ourselves. The atmosphere of the ancient town was tangible as we walked along those cart-rutted, deserted streets, unchanged, apart obviously from the damage, since AD 79. Houses with colourful wall paintings, seemed full of the ghosts of their long gone inhabitants. Many of these decorations were as fresh as the day they were painted and many had distinctly humorous and extremely vulgar subject matter.

"I think I can guess what they're looking at," Harry said, as we noticed a small gathering of laughing people peering up at a wall. And of course we had to look too.

The morning was hot and still. Vesuvius could be seen shimmering in the distance; a serial killer with the face of an angel. It did not seem at all possible that something so far away and so beautiful could have caused such destruction. Surrounded by this air of quiet mystery we were suddenly brought back to reality by the inevitable: an influx of several large coach-loads of tourists. In an effort to keep their parties together, the Dutch waved flags and the Japanese brandished umbrellas, and those antique cobbled streets now took on the air of Notting Hill during the carnival. The spell of ancient Pompeii now seemed as comprehensively broken as its walls. Still, at least we had been privileged to experience something of this special place on our own terms, even if it had been for only a short time. We were lucky that we could travel independently, rather than having to rely on being herded from one famous site to the next with hardly a pause for thought in between.

During our travels, we shunned eating stuff brought from home, (the camping and caravanning magazines were full of recipes for canned cuisine) preferring to sample the abundant fresh vegetables available locally wherever we went. This meant that the cooking process took a bit longer, but was always one of the highlights of the day. We were spoilt for choice, particularly in Italy, but when it came to fresh mushrooms this was not always the case. Obviously they are a problem in hotter climates, which explains the prevalence of the dried type, but we never let the challenge of locating an unusual ingredient defeat us. This attitude also applied to things that went wrong in the campervan, which is how we got to know many a town while trawling the streets for various parts. We seldom failed. Parma was scoured not for its ham or cheese, but a belt for the tape player, Segovia, glow plugs for the engine. Both missions were successful and in the process we got to know the places almost inside out. At Pompeii, mushrooms were the small objects of desire.

Our quest for this essential ingredient began later that day when we decided to take the bus to the shops in the 'new' town. This was where we were discovered by our Pompeian canine stalker. He had been curled up in that familiar ball in the shade of a shop-awning when he took a shine to us as we passed by. Maybe we should have just ignored him, but this was difficult. Each time we crossed a road he was so convinced we were his, that he blindly followed us over and we found ourselves turning round to check that he was still in one piece.

"If we speed up, we might lose him," I said hopefully.

I did not relish the responsibility of getting a dog run over even if he was smelly and mangy. But he matched our new pace perfectly.

"Well maybe he'll give up when we go into this shop!"

Harry grabbed my arm and swerved me skilfully into the cool, white-tiled and pristine *Mozzarella* shop we were passing. I was convinced that the squeaky clean girl standing behind the counter in her immaculate white overall recoiled when she saw the spectre sitting patiently outside like the ghost of *Banquo*.

"We'd only need a to attach him to a piece of string and we'd look like vagrants," I said, ignoring the fact that we in no way resembled those unfortunates seen inhabiting London shop doorways.

To allow a dog to get in such an awful condition would be an offence in the UK and I hated the idea that anyone would assume we were his owners. There was no escaping the accusing stares of locals though, as we queued outside a small supermarket waiting for it to open. At last the doors were unlocked, and we dashed inside. Emerging stealthily a little while later, we looked to left and right.

"Well, has our little friend given up?" I asked hopefully.

"I can't see him," Harry replied, "he's probably found some other likely-looking suckers to follow."

I felt guilty to be so relieved, but there were so many of these pathetic creatures around the place, what were we to do?

Back at the campsite, an altogether more agreeable 'doggy' encounter took place. A cute puppy, one of the many strays we'd become aware of hanging round the site, had been loitering close to the van since we'd relocated that morning. Harry, not well known as a dog lover, made the mistake of offering it one of my precious '*Hobnobs*'.

"I've been rationing those biscuits so they last until we get back," I complained. "You'll never get rid of him now."

He thought we were his new family. It was difficult to resist his charms since he had the appeal of those cuddly pups in the loo-roll ads.

"Shall we take him home with us?" I thought Harry was joking, but I wasn't sure.

The young however are fickle. They are more interested in their stomachs than any kind of loyalty, and our little friend's allegiance soon switched to our German neighbours on discovering they had something even more to his taste. Biscuits just could not compete with *brätwurst*. Such a delicacy was like *Ambrosia*, the food of the gods, to that little stray on the *Campeggio Zeus*. With this offering, he thought he was in paradise, though I can't remember if we ourselves managed to obtain our idea of heaven – fresh mushrooms.

Venice: Vaporetti and Victimisation

As George Orwell might have put it:
All campers are equal but some are more equal than others.
It seems that even in the ostensibly egalitarian world of camping, there may be an occult hierarchy operating. Those in charge of *Campeggio Miramare,* at the Venice lagoon port of *Punta Sabbioni,* had certainly taken on board that much quoted mantra.

We did not expect to like Venice. In some ways we'd resisted going there. All the hype was off-putting and the popular belief that the water is smelly and the place unpleasantly crammed full of tourists didn't help. However, when you don't expect much, you're usually in for a pleasant surprise. Venice therefore, far exceeded our expectations. In late June the canal waters were inoffensive, and neither did we see any of the famous dead dogs floating in them. At times there were not even that many tourists, particularly earlier in the day before the coach loads arrived from distant towns.

It's a place unique in a way that most other unique cities are not: the pedestrian is king. No dodging those nippy Lambretta's or breathing in noxious traffic fumes; just the unalloyed pleasure of strolling round the alleyways, getting lost at times but not really caring. We thought Venice was great, but the proprietors of our chosen campsite on the Venice Lagoon didn't share that opinion about our campervan.

Punta Sabbioni is at the end of the long curving spit of land to the east of Venice, that encloses the Lagoon from the Adriatic. To get there one has to be determined. Once reaching the outskirts of the city itself, you have to completely ignore it and carry on eastwards in the direction of Trieste, the place Churchill once designated as being the start of the so-called 'Iron Curtain'. If you've just driven from the South, this is particularly frustrating as you then watch the signs for Venice point back to where you've just come from. You then take the westward road along the road towards Punta Sabbioni. It was along this road that a myriad of campsites beckoned us like Sirens to end our hot and tiring journey in their swimming pools or seaside lidos. They were difficult to resist. Every junction had a sign indicating the number of sites to the left, right or ahead, and it was staggering how many there were in such a small area.

Harry became impatient to stop for the day,

"I hope this site of yours is worth passing all those others for."

"Well don't blame me if it isn't. Blame that magazine!"

I prayed I'd been right to insist we kept *right on to the end of the road,* as the numbers went down till there was only one left: my chosen destination. A reader's recommendation in a motorhome magazine had tempted me, not only for its convenient position near the *traghetto* terminal for visiting the city, but by the tempting description of:

"Grassy, generously-sized and hedge-enclosed pitches providing the kind of lushness and privacy which was usually in short supply elsewhere".

Most places we chose to stay on gave us free reign to pitch where we wanted, but we didn't mind that *Campeggio Miramare* allocated us a pitch because of these exciting advantages. When it turned out that the place we were sent to was not in any way "grassy" or "generously-sized" we were a bit miffed. The "hedge-enclosed" part of the description turned out to be a few straggly bits of privet. Maybe in a few years' time these twigs would form an adequate hedge for a pygmy to hide behind, but when we were there even an emaciated mouse would have been hard pushed to find any cover.

"This isn't exactly my idea of privacy," I said

My observant Other Half had also found something else was missing:

"And where's all that grassy lushness?"

The ground was sand. And you could hardly call the few struggling grass-stalks "lush".

We began to doubt the veracity of that magazine reader.

"He must have got carried away by greed to win that ten quid," I suggested.

That evening, we took a stroll round the site. The *lush* pieces of real estate we discovered were situated at the far side, and mainly occupied by shiny new caravans and motor homes. We observed that a more *mature* age-group had the monopoly of the place.

"Looks like they've been spending their childrens' inheritances," Harry remarked.

Through the gaps in those lovely green hedges, we could see a couple of silver haired travellers outside each unit drinking mugs of tea on their verdant lawns. Interestingly, not all of the 'vans were brand spanking new, but none of the tenants were come to that.

Well at least we could reassure ourselves, by way of consolation, that the site operators gave us the benefit of youth if nothing else. That our lowly quarter of *Campeggio Miramare* was occupied by somewhat younger, less regimented residents was flattering in a way. I couldn't help but feel insulted though that even if they thought we weren't old enough, we weren't good enough for their best pitches either. To add insult to injury, the swankier area also boasted a pristine new shower and toilet block.

"Do you think they pay more for those pitches?" I wondered.

"Well as we weren't given the option, I doubt it."

After living on the site for a couple of days we eventually found out the truth about the suspected apartheid. Twice since our arrival we'd decided to change pitches. The first time was because quite reasonably, we didn't wish to reside right next to the toilet block (the old and shabby one) when there were clearly other spaces available. Apart from the smell, the sound of doors banging and loos being flushed through the night is not conducive to good sleep.

A combination of things instigated our second move. Initially there was the Italian equivalent of the *'Simpson'* family behind us, whose children insisted on using our space both as a cut through to their own van and as the outfield of their football pitch. Despite us being in the middle of an *al fresco* meal, they thought it quite normal to kick their ball under our dining table – well the collapsible picnic one anyway. Stringing up a line of towels between us and them should have given the message that we weren't occupying a public footpath or the *Juventis* stadium, but they still didn't take the hint. They merely shoved their way through my clean towels with their grubby hands. But then the parents seemed just as bad as their offspring. On top of all the physical intrusion, our ears were also constantly being bashed. A TV outside their van blared out the most atrocious trash from morning 'till night, and when Homer, Bart and co. were not stuffing their faces or re-enacting the Italia '90 World Cup, the only other family activities seemed to be wrestling, arguing and shouting.

We'd been lucky enough to have a lovely young New Zealand couple, Murray and Fiona, next to us, but unfortunately they'd already been there a few days and were due to move on. A camper van full of German chain smokers replaced them and we knew it was time for us to have yet another change of pitch. The Kiwis had been pleasant company, but our new 'neighbours' now made it impossible to sit outside at any time of day. Even Bart and co weren't that annoying.

Harry found himself returning to the reception yet again to get another pitch. Despite there still being spaces in the elite quarter, this time we were allocated somewhere amid the even humbler tents of back-packers, but the air was clear, the occupants pleasant and it was peaceful, even though we were now of course in the least favourable part nearest to the road.

One of the site organisers, did a nightly round on his bicycle to check that all was well, and that night he stopped to ask if we were now satisfied with our pitch.

"*Scusi*. Why you want move so many times?"

This was the perfect opportunity for us to confirm our suspicions as to why we'd continually been given the 'bum' parts of the site to stay on.

"So why haven't you given us a place on the hedged part of the site?" Harry dared to ask.

The friendly *signor* shrugged his shoulders.

"There are vacant places there," my hero pointed out.

Pressed, the man had to concede:

"These are for *a certain sort of van*," he admitted.

"Newer and more expensive vans you mean?"

The man shrugged his shoulders again. "Well, you could say that."

"And do they pay more than us?"

Yet again those shoulders rose and fell, but he couldn't wriggle out of it. At least we knew for sure now. My hackles, whatever they are, began to rise.

"I'm going to write to all the camping and caravanning publications in England to warn people not to come here unless they want to be treated like second class citizens!"

I threatened this with as much menace as I could muster, which at five feet tall probably was not much. If this bothered him in the slightest he didn't make it obvious. There were visitors to the site from all over the world, it was after all so convenient. Any reduction in numbers brought about by my threat would be as insignificant as a drop taken out of the ocean.

This kind of apartheid was the first we'd knowingly encountered, but as is usual when I threaten to "write to *someone* about *something*" it was an empty threat. By the time we were home, I simply couldn't be bothered. Instead I found consolation in the idea that we'd not been identified as a pair of old fogies like those smug, £10-winning caravanners who'd recommended *Campeggio Miramare* in the first place.

Murray and Fiona, had told us about the wonderful evening they'd passed in Venice. The city, they said, is not interested in catering for night-clubbers, so once most of the tourists have gone, the bands playing under the canopies outside the expensive *Piazza San Marco* restaurants provide entertainment for those left behind. They apparently competed in a kind of musical sparring match, each trying to outdo the other with a virtuoso performance. We liked the sound of this, and with the ferries operating throughout the night, we planned an evening visit on our final day. Unfortunately or trip was thwarted by a terrific thunder storm breaking out just before setting off, so instead of catching the boat, we stood under an umbrella on the shore outside the campsite and in the torrential rain, watched the lightening over the distant Venetian skyline. Turner had depicted Venice during one of these storms, and I would never have believed then that one day a few years later, I would stand in the basement of the Edinburgh National Gallery actually holding this famous painting in my hands – but that, as they say, is another story.

Despite the storm, the evening was balmy, so we returned to the van and sat outside under the awning, drinks in hand, to storm-watch. A young German couple had set up a small tent next to us before the rain started, leaving immediately to catch the ferry into Venice. We noticed they'd left their foam bed rolls outside the tent presumably to 'air', but now these were in danger of becoming rather damp.

"We can't just sit and watch their bedding get soaked," Harry said, "I'll roll it up and put it in their tent." I preferred to keep myself to myself, but Harry is more thoughtful, and got a soaking himself as a reward.

"I bet they won't even realise you've done them a favour," I said.

When they turned up later, they didn't notice anything different.

With the Grand Canal never far away and our return boat never too long in the waiting, Venice was the perfect place to explore without the usual problems associated with large cities. The cheapness and frequency of the *vaporetti* that travel the length of the Grand Canal added to the charm of the place, and we spent much of our time there like five-year-olds, enjoying the novelty of hopping on and off them.

On one occasion, whilst waiting at a landing stage, we were being closely observed by a thin and wizened but smartly-dressed elderly gentleman. He appeared to be a local, and to my over-suspicious mind seemed a bit too interested in us for comfort. Harry as a rule has no qualms about getting to know the natives of anywhere we may be visiting, although he usually favours those of the young female variety. Being stared at in this way by a stranger was disconcerting even to him though. As we alighted into the more enclosed space of the water-bus, the dapper *signor* took this as his cue to begin quizzing us.

"You Ingleesh?" he asked.

"You leeve near Cornwall?"

"How long you stay uh?"

"I travel in Ingland many time. I have friend in Cornwall. You know zis Cornwall, uh?"

When we established that we didn't in fact live in that county, he wanted to know exactly where we lived, so we told him.

"I can veesit you no? On ze island of white yes? I can veesit on way to Cornwall?"

He produced a little black book from his inside pocket.

"You draw map for me. Show where is Island,"

Harry duly drew a rough map of the UK with the little diamond shape of the Isle of Wight at the bottom. He demurred from adding our address to the page though, not relishing the thought of having either an unwanted surprise guest in the future or a gang of international house-breakers entering our unoccupied home in the present.

"Unfortunately the Island is quite difficult to get to from where you're going,"

This was not entirely a fib. It's hardly on the way to anywhere except of course France, and then only if you catch the boat from Portsmouth first and jump off to swim ashore in Ryde. Clearly not easily put off by this, when we arrived at the *Rialto* vaporetto stop it was obvious our friend intended to stick with us. It took a deft bit of footwork worthy of Fred Astaire to give him the slip. We didn't wish to be rude, so having politely wished him *"arrivederci"*, without waiting for a reply, Harry extravagantly pointed in direction of the bridge as if to go that way, only to grab my arm and rush me off the opposite way. As we disappeared into the milling crowd of canal-side tourists, our elderly companion didn't stand a chance of catching us up in that scrum.

Back in the safety of the campsite later that day, I was idly looking through my guidebooks to decide where we should visit the following morning, when I was taken aback by a warning in one of them.

"Oh--my--goodness! It says here to be wary of strangers trying to befriend you on the *vaporetti*!"

"You what? Why?"

"It doesn't say why. There's no reason given. But it's there in black and white if you don't believe me!"

I showed him the book.

Was our aspiring houseguest part of some conspiracy or merely an innocent with a particular interest in the most south-westerly county of England? If anyone mentions Cornwall to you during a trip to Venice though – you might also wish to utilise a few Fred Astaire moves to avoid unwanted visitors in the future.

"All Of Our Pitches Are Flat"

"Vere is he going?" asked the woman in charge, poking her head menacingly out of the door.

Although it was quite obvious, I refrained from saying anything sarcastic or flippant, so I just replied in my friendliest way,

"He's looking for a flat pitch,"

"He should haf vaited for my permission. Anyway, all of our pitches are flat,"

Unfortunately for us, we'd mistaken her arm-waving acknowledgement in our direction as we drove in as 'permission' to enter the site. In our defence, we'd found it was often the case on these little French sites that the owners waved us through not worrying unduly about checking us in first. But then this site was run by a couple from the Netherlands.

After filling the forms in triplicate, I was still feeling embarrassed at being ticked off, and in a bid to gain her good opinion, I ordered an exorbitantly over-priced loaf for the following morning. It was our misfortune not to have read the sign by the entrance giving chapter and verse on how to enter the site appropriately and what not to do whilst there. Having been on the road since 10 o'clock that day and after 5 hours of travelling, the last thing we were interested in was a list of *don'ts* as long as your arm.

We came to realise that even though they are charming, well-educated and speak perfect English, some people from Holland lacked our sense of the ridiculous and the British dislike of unnecessary rules: *"Rules are made for the guidance of the wise and the obeyance of the stupid,"* was Harry's favourite saying.

This site in the Dordogne was home to the King and Queen of rule-makers. It was mind-blowing how many they'd managed to think up for obstructing would-be bathers from using their swimming pool. Signboards with lists of 'dos and don'ts' considerately translated into several languages, were attached to the fence enclosing the otherwise attractive facility. However because the boards were so numerous, they stretched most of the way round the pool area, making the need for an actual fence redundant – except of course to hold the boards. These stipulations were so all-encompassing, that we doubted if anyone had actually qualified to enter the water, ever. The owners of course had every right to eject anyone not coming up to their fastidious criteria, and they did have a point in not wanting anything nasty entering their pool

Once we'd established ourselves on site, I decided that as the afternoon was warm and the pool was open – quite a novelty in our experience – I'd go for a swim.

"Are you sure you qualify?" Harry joked.

"I doubt it, but I'll see what happens."

I was sort of confident that I was free from all those illnesses and diseases, and being equipped with suitable attire to comply with decency (also mentioned), I crept past the signboards. The proprietor and her other half were now on sun-loungers at the side of the water, magazines placed strategically on their laps. In their reflective sunglasses though, it was difficult to tell if they were actually reading or instead spying on anyone having the nerve to try out their leisure facility. Those rule-boards were making me paranoid. I plunged into the cool water: a welcome diversion on such a hot day. But I can't say this was the most relaxing swim of my life. Apart from those four eyes searing through the sun-block on my back, I was accompanied in the water by a flotilla of floating insects. They'd had no problem flouting the rules.

"Maybe the proprietors should have spent some of the signboard money on a decent filtering system," I said under my breath, as I joined Harry on the grass outside the *verboden* area. I discreetly attempted to make sense of the rules again from underneath the towel while I rubbed my hair. It was no wonder the pool was empty: we began to think that maybe for the same reason, the site was too.

But the pitches were all *very* flat - which brings us to Holland.

On a site just outside Amsterdam, it was even more difficult to please the fearsome woman running the place. She had already intimidated me (not difficult) along with several young people who'd turned up in reception after us. Once everyone had been put in their place – metaphorically – she jumped on her bike to lead us to our pitch. Well this *was* Amsterdam. Fine, we thought. No chance of misunderstandings. But as Harry drove onto the marked-out grassy area, just to park on the correct pitch turned out not to be good enough.

"No, No, NO!!!! You must face ze uzzer vay!" she commanded, like an exasperated sergeant major in charge of a raw recruit.

My Other Half did not take kindly to being ordered about like this but in the interests of International harmony, he patiently turned the van round. Only it was still not right.

"You must be more over to ze left!" she was really getting into her stride now, "You must haf zis much space on zis side", and she held out her hands about 18 inches apart.

If only we had a tape-measure on us, we could have made a point, but luckily we didn't. After a lot of shunting about Harry turned the engine off. He'd had enough of wasting all that expensive diesel. If she wasn't satisfied now, it was too bad.

"Why does it need to be so precisely positioned?" he had the nerve to ask.

"It is ze rules!" she retorted, and realising she'd met her match, gave a loud "Humph", jumped on her bike and pedalled back towards reception. No doubt she intended taking it out on those cowering young back-packers awaiting her return.

We surveyed our surroundings. Caravans and motor caravans were laid out in geometric precision good enough to make the marines proud. Each was at the exact angle facing *outwards*, in a fan-like shape matching the curve of the perimeter road. Heaven help us! It really was like being in a military camp. Enclosed by this semi-circle of vehicles was the tent area, another military camp if ever I saw one. Though unfortunately for the predilections our hostess, these were in a myriad of colours rather than khaki.

But apart from all this rule business, generally we found Dutch citizens to be amiable and gregarious in their own quiet manner. Commuters on the Amsterdam subway were keen to practise their English on us, speaking it so well we felt ashamed we knew nothing of their language. They did re-assure us though that Dutch was tricky even for them!

I loved Amsterdam's *Rijksmuseum*. During a visit to the London National Gallery once, I was almost thrown out for attempting to take a photo from the window towards Trafalgar Square *outside* from one of the stairways. What harm that would have done I've no idea. In contrast, the *Rijksmuseum* permitted photography everywhere, allowing me to strike a pose with the lads of 'The Night-Watch', along with *Vermeers* and other *Rembrandts* that were all there for the 'taking'.

Maybe it was just Dutch people on campsites who were so keen on rules and regulations. But they really *do* have extremely flat pitches, even in the Dordogne.

Willcommen, Bienvenido, Welcome

"This is not passport. This is pass for bus."

The poker-faced girl at the audio-guide desk was in no mood to appreciate what she thought was a joke. Well, who could blame her really. It was unbearably hot, even inside the *Alcazar* in Seville, and the party of school kids in front of us had probably already given her enough cheek for one day.

We didn't like giving away our passports to anyone. We thought this quite reasonable seeing as we felt so far from home. Unfortunately people in charge of campsites and ticket offices did not share our misgivings, and were always trying to prise them out of our clammy possession.

Since there was an audio guide in English available for the *Alcázar*, we thought it would be worth taking advantage of. If they'd wanted us to pledge a kidney as security to stop us running off with it, we might not have hesitated. Well we both had two of those. But organ donation was not on their wish-list: it was passports they wanted and we only had one each of these. The flimsy box in which they were storing other people's deposits didn't look too safe in our opinion, and this was why Harry thought his Identity card for the Isle of Wight catamaran would be a good substitute. But the girl was not having any of it.

"You cannot use zis thing," she said blankly, "Is not passport."

"Oh for goodness sake," I moaned, "I'll give her **my** passport and we can share."

I just had to hope that this wouldn't be the day raiders would choose to sneak round the back and grab the box of goodies.

As we returned the headset to the desk after our tour – slightly prolonged by having to explain to each other what we'd just heard on each part of the commentary – our old sparring partner had been transformed into Miss Congeniality. Even though the smile looked a little false, we welcomed the improvement.

"Did you like visit?" She almost gushed, but not quite.

"Err, yes thank you."

"Yes eet is very lovely place, no? Much history. You like Seville?" The change of attitude was almost painful.

We thanked her very much, re-gained my passport (luckily not seized in a raid), thanked our new best friend again and went on our way. We were left wondering whether the place was run with robots and this one had developed a fault. While we were wandering round the *Alcázar*, the circuits had been changed.

Spain did not seem to have quite got the idea of how to welcome foreigners. Museum custodians were content to prop up walls whilst chatting to co-workers, or colleagues as they used to be known in simpler times, sharing a joke and a fag. Any unsuspecting tourist butted in on their socialising at his or her peril. If you wanted to know where something was, you were directed to someone else who in turn … well you get the idea.

Some campsite receptionists had perfected this onerous business of meeting and greeting. A young lady working at a site north of Córdoba was an expert. It was amazing to behold and I marvelled at her skill for days after.

Being low season, she wasn't exactly rushed off her feet as I entered the neat reception building.

"¡Hola! Buenos tardes," though I was exhausted by the long hot slog through the wasteland at the centre of Spain, to be polite was no more effort than being off-hand.

Silence.

"*Por favore. Uno Camping Car. Por favore,*"

More silence.

At the very least she could have acknowledged my existence on the other side of the counter. I mean, I know I'm short, but not that short.

Without even a glance or a nod in my direction, she took my credit card and camping card, tapped something into a keyboard, put the cards back on the counter, and printed-up a receipt which was slapped on the top of them. In the room behind her were several other young people and a TV blaring out some atrocious, noisy game-show. If she managed to avoid conversation with me during the transaction, Miss Congeniality 2 did manage to keep up the banter with her friends.

"*Muchas gracias,*" I hoped I didn't sound too sarcastic, but when the usual "*De nada*" wasn't forthcoming, I hoped I did.

And 'have a nice day' to you too!

Of course, there is always a shiny side to the tarnished coin of customer relations. If Seville's *alcázar* had the frostiest receptionist, this city was home to the friendliest policeman and the kindliest shop assistant.

Like any large city, Seville's road system is manic and confusing for anyone new to it. Even locals might get into trouble if they relax their guard for a milli-second. We were driving along the beautiful palm-lined and aptly named *Avenida de las Delicias,* in pursuit of a car park. There were plenty around, but unfortunately they were all underground with height restrictions barring us from their cool protection. Soon the *delicious* avenue turned into a foul, four-laned, one-way vision of hell and then decided to split itself in two. After a few circuits of Valhalla, we decided to pull over and consult our street plan. All those car parks were shown, but none seemed to indicate that it was above ground. From the corner of my eye I saw a figure approach. A figure in uniform. A figure with a gun glinting at his side in the bright Spanish sunlight.

"We'd better move," I hinted.

Harry wound down the window.

"Hola! You Ingleesh? May I 'elp?"

Not only did he speak English and wasn't in a rush to move us on, he wasn't threatening us with a ticket either. Or that gun.

"We're looking for a car park. One that's not underground,"

"Oh sure," he said. "You 'ave map, yes? There is car park for you next to Bull Ring."

Of course, the Bull Ring – the one made famous by Bizet's opera Carmen. If we'd picked the other fork in the Delicias we'd have found it. As we had an immense dislike for the idea of a bull-fight, and no intention of visiting the place, we'd chosen to avoid it.

"Where you are from Eengland?"

Harry reached for our GB map and showed him the Isle of Wight, and then produced the well-thumbed Michelin maps to trace our journey down through France and to the south of Spain.

He laughed. "You long way from 'ome!"

"Just a bit!"

"I 'elp you now. Good-day!"

He saluted, and like a fearless David, strode out in front of the Philistine onslaught and held up his arms. Four lines of speeding traffic screeched to a halt. He turned and gallantly beckoned to us to move out. So this is how it feels to be royalty.

"Muchas gracias," we called. What a lovely man.

It was also in Seville that I caught the Flamenco bug. Not from seeing a performance, but from seeing the colourful and beautifully flounced, over-the-top dresses in boutique windows around the city centre. Rather than a dress though - the prices I felt must have mistakenly had too many noughts put on the end - I decided to treat myself to a pair of shoes. Shoes are my thing. I love shoes. And well, you never know when you might need a pair to dance the Flamenco do you?

We entered a little narrow shop. I didn't know where to look first. I was surrounded by shoes, fans, dresses and castanets. An attractive young lady with long blonde hair was just finishing serving another customer, and turned her attention to us. I explained that I wanted some Flamenco shoes, told her my size and she disappeared into the dark recesses of a back room. She returned with a few pairs for me to try but I felt like one of Cinderella's step-sisters being challenged by a glass slipper. It appears that small feet are not a characteristic of the average Spanish female.

"Lo siento. Ees only ones in shop,"

Harry could see my disappointment.

"Why not get yourself a fan instead?"

I was determined to have something genuine to remember Seville by, rather than a tacky tourist souvenir, so this seemed an excellent suggestion. Now I had the poor girl producing fans from several drawers around the shop, and of course the decision of which to buy was agonising. Eventually I decided on a black one, with hand-painted flowers both on the wood and on the fabric. It was beautiful. She painstakingly replaced it in the box and wrapped it in tissue, adding a ribbon as the finishing touch.

"Do you know where we could see a Flamenco performance?" Harry asked.

"Of course! I will write for you," and she carefully made a list of all the times and places where we could find a show that day.

Now this little shopping episode may be quite unremarkable, but it was only when we went to leave the boutique that we noticed the time. Seville's siesta, like any other Mediterranean town or city, started at noon at the very latest. It was now past 12.30. As that kind and patient young woman locked the door behind us, we realised she had not once looked at her watch or tried to make me get a move on with my decision making.

"You wouldn't get that kind of service on the Isle of Wight."

There, just in case anyone dares to make a last minute purchase, they always lock the doors at least five minutes before closing time. Sometimes ten.

Mind you, Isle of Wight shopkeepers don't pull the shutters down for the whole afternoon either. We just don't have the weather to justify siestas.

Apes, Rocks and Pizza
The Ins and Outs of Gibraltar

"It lay apart like an interloper, as though it had been towed out from Portsmouth and anchored off-shore still wearing its own grey roof of weather...

...Leaving Gibraltar was like escaping from an elder brother in charge of an open jail."
Laurie Lee - 'As I walked Out One Midsummer Morning'

Disappointingly for me or maybe luckily for us, the day we arrived at Gibraltar it had thrown off that grey roof and the sun was shining. But *Gib* was as awkward a customer as when Laurie went there in the early 1930s.

Fellow travellers on *Camping Chullera* near *Manilva* on the coast to the North-East of the Rock, had given us a dilemma.

"Don't take your van into Gibraltar!"

"Whatever you do, don't leave the van outside!"

The town of *San Roque* at the entrance point to the Rock, we were assured, was a den of drug addicts who found easy pickings by breaking into vehicles parked by those visiting the British Colony on foot. As all we had was in our van, we did not relish the thought of losing any of it but on the other hand, there was also good reason not to drive into the place. We might find it difficult to leave. On a whim, we were told, the temperamental Spanish customs officers often decided to hold up vehicles quitting Gibraltar, or to put it another way, those wishing to re-enter Spain. This resulted in motorists sitting in their vehicles for an unspecified length of time both at their mercy and that of the relentless sunshine. Needless to say, neither scenario appealed to us, but we were determined that having gone all that way, driving past was not an option. After all, apart from its significance to me because of Laurie Lee's visit, Gibraltar's historical significance meant that even my travel-weary Other Half was keen to go there.

After much deliberation, we decided to risk leaving the van in Spain rather than later fry in the sun for several hours. Our doors were, after all, on a vehicle meant to withstand rough use by workmen rather than the loving care of a holiday-home owner. The robust nature of our *Leyland Daf* conversion meant that breaking into it would be a tad tricky, assuming someone thought it worth attempting in the first place. Added to this, the road next to the border was busy with people and traffic, and several yellow-baseball-cap-and-yellow-jerkined officials could be seen patrolling the area. We assumed their task was to check that people had bought a parking ticket from the roadside meters. The price of a ticket seemed a small one to pay for peace of mind due to the presence of these attendants and also for the avoidance of the possible hot and lengthy wait to get back across the border later.

I found a ticket machine, and attempted to put some coins in it. Soon a couple of young English women joined me and between us we tried to make sense of the instructions. Our small gathering attracted one of the men in yellow.

"Parking - Sabado - Is free!" The gap-toothed, weather-beaten face beamed at us. How kind and helpful.

"What a great place!" we all agreed, thanking him.

Before leaving the van, we drew the curtains and left the radio on in an attempt to make out it was occupied: we just hoped we'd made the right decision.

Getting into Gibraltar was easy, but soon the similarity with an old-fashioned British Sunday became apparent. Everything was shut. Even the famous cable car going up to see the even more famous apes, was not running. It looked like too long and strenuous a walk to attempt on that sweltering day, and while we stood dithering about what to do, we were approached by one of the local taxi drivers.

"May I help you?" he said in an accent not exactly Spanish, but not exactly English either. "If you wish to visit the Rock, I can take you,"

We normally preferred getting a local bus than doing the 'touristy' thing of getting taxis anywhere, but these were exceptional circumstances. Negotiating the cost, we agreed to take him up on the trip, but setting off up the steep and winding slope, we wondered if we'd chosen wisely. Our driver was a charming and friendly man, but we held onto our unbelted seats in the back of his cab as he drove at break-neck speed towards the summit, rounding each bend on two wheels.

It was a relief when midway, he stopped the car at the entrance to some caves. This labyrinth we discovered was once used by the military for lookout posts and garrisons.

"This is very interesting," he said, "you maybe like to visit?"

Well of course we did, even though certain that he was rewarded for each tourist he dropped off there. But we didn't mind. As our eyes became accustomed to the darkness inside, it was amazing to be surrounded by weird and spectacular formations of stalactites and stalagmites, some resembling elaborate chandeliers, others fantastical creatures. Further along, corridors hewn into the rock gave views over the indigo blue *Straights* and we snatched our first glimpse Africa, so near yet so far. Hazy purple-blue mountains rose mysteriously on the horizon. I hadn't expected that, though what exactly I had expected I wasn't sure.

We came out blinking into the daylight at a spot further along and there was our driver who greeted us like long-lost friends. He'd been sitting in a café at the cave exit, drinking coffee – well nothing stronger we hoped - having a smoke and a chat to his fellow drivers while we did the tourist thing. It seemed a perfect arrangement for everyone.

Next came more of that seat-gripping to our next stop. This was the thing I'd most been looking forward to - the hang-out of those Gibraltarian clichés, the Barbary Apes. So you can see I was more than a bit disappointed to find that rather than the cuddly tea-drinking chimps I'd been expecting, these were the most vicious creatures ever let loose onto an unsuspecting public. Petrified children from a German family ahead of us were being attacked for the sweets in their pockets. Even the baby apes had teeth to compete in sharpness and number with that hideous creature in the film *Alien*. I cowered as far away as I could, terrified that I might get attacked: every time one of them looked in my direction, my screams were loud enough to cause panic across the *straights*. I couldn't get away quick enough.

Thankfully much further along, and from the vantage point of the highest part of the Rock, we were thrilled to peer through the telescope and see our van parked on the distant road, its mustard paintwork glimmering in the mid-day sun, and so tiny it could have been a dinky toy. That it was still there caused a joint sigh of relief.

By the time we arrived back at base in the main part of town, we were ready to sample the local fare. But in keeping with that old-fashioned British tradition, apart from smoke-filled pubs, the only place open was a *Pizza* parlour. So we settled for an Italian meal in this British colony on the Spanish coast. And very good it was too.

Walking back towards the border across the runway serving the airport, we were still a little anxious about having left our home parked outside at the mercy of passing felons. With the sun fiercer than when we'd entered *Gib* hours before, we breezed unhindered through the air-conditioned customs building, on foot. A three-lane queue of cars was melting into the tarmac outside. It seemed we really had made the right decision after all. Our little home awaited us, untouched, and ready to make a quick getaway.

Feeling victorious, we left Gibraltar behind and headed for the scene of another more famous victory: Cape Trafalgar.

Fuentes!
...and a diary of our final days in Spain

By the latter part of our Spanish Odyssey the conversation in our van's intimate interior usually goes something like this:

Him : "Well where do you want to go next?"

Me: "Well I'd hoped to go to *abc*."

Him: "How far is it?"

Me: "About *xyz* miles."

Him: "Well is it on our way?"

Me: "Not directly."

Him: "What's there? I'm not driving 100 miles out of our way to see another *alcazar* if that's what you think."

Me: "An *Alcazar* and a church."

Him: "Haven't you seen enough?"

Me: "They do look rather nice in the guidebook!"

Him: "I thought you wanted to go to Paris on the way back to the tunnel."

Me: "We won't be coming back here, so it's my only chance. We can always do Paris another time."

In fact we've 'done' Paris quite a few times already. Admittedly one alcazar is starting to look much like another and the sight of a badly painted Murillo-type Virgin gazing up ecstatically from a musty chapel is beginning to pall. Occasionally I see sense and give in, but not too often.

Following unswervingly in the footsteps of my hero is not going exactly to plan even if it had been part of the plan in the first place.

For a start, our time in Spain begins in the Eastern Pyrenees rather than on the Atlantic North-West coast of the country. To 'do' this vast country in three to four weeks even on wheels, would be almost impossible and there's only so much history and travelling that one can cope with. There are however, those places described so lucidly in the book that I cannot not leave Spain without seeing.

One such place is *La Granja*, the palace of a former king of Spain at *San Ildefonso*, north of the *Sierra de Guadarrama*. Coming across it unexpectedly, Laurie finds the place deserted apart from gardeners seemingly awaiting the return of a long-dead monarch, going about their business awaiting further instruction. Was it this scenario that inspired the final scene of *Silent Running,* we wonder. In the film, robots, as space-age gardeners, continue to tend the precious trees once the humans have departed. Into infinity and beyond…

It was not merely the inexplicably deserted nature of the place that beguiled Laurie: water featured throughout the grounds to rival even Versailles and any way it could be spouted, trickled and splashed was employed. *La Granja* is too tempting.

By the time we cross the *Sierra Guadarrama* towards *Segovia*, Harry and even myself to a certain extent have become travel weary, and maybe in consequence disillusioned with Spain. He had declared himself "*alcazared* out" a hundred miles or so before, and it is with relief that we are now travelling north across the surprisingly green and alpine *Puerto de Navacerrado* to our final intended destination in the country.

Monday 14th June

We find *La Granja* easily, but of course it being Monday, we are greeted by locked gates. What happens in Spain on a Monday? Does everyone there have such a hedonistic weekend that they need an extra day to recover? By now we are used to such disappointments, and decide to drive the few extra miles up the road to Segovia, stay there and return to the gardens when they open on Wednesday.

After all, hadn't my idol stayed in an inn under the Roman aqueduct there? We could 'kill' two *Laurie Lee birds* with one stone, something that doesn't happen too often.

Our stay in Segovia is largely uneventful. Missing by one day a torrential downpour flash-flooding the campsite, the deluge has disappeared as quickly as it came. The usual quest to find somewhere to purchase some obscure object for the van (this time new *glow plugs* - the diesel equivalent to spark plugs apparently) takes up much of our first day there, resulting in us getting to know the town and its commercial enterprises quite well. Those selling car spares being the least fascinating. In an effort to get somewhere before the big lunchtime shutdown I'm forced to bypass many a more interesting boutique, but we are becoming experts on the whereabouts of motor mechanic's workshops though. To give them their due, the proprietors there are far more helpful than their British equivalents. Overcoming extreme language difficulties, we have the satisfaction of tracking down these latest small objects of desire and can now look forward hopefully to a trouble-free return journey northwards.

Tuesday 15th June

Segovia's aqueduct is everything I'd hoped it would be, apart from there being no trace of Laurie's inn under its protection. Of course it was a long time since he'd been there, and we get the feeling that a recent clean-up might explain the pristine condition of the area. The locals in time-honoured fashion, do not seem to be as impressed as we are with this ancient feature which strides so magnificently through their city. I'm horrified to see a wizened, beret-wearing elder of the place using it as a base for chopping his firewood: the sound bouncing off of those vast antique stone arches like an eerie echo of the masons at work two millennia before.

As evening creeps in, the central *plaza* which lies in the shadow of this vast structure, becomes the focus of the evening *passeo*.

Huge and black like a *Goya* Colossus against the backdrop of the reddening sky, the amazing piece of Roman ingenuity soars proudly and protectively above the locals who are busily chatting and posing in their finest attire. Being more concerned with outdoing the neighbours by parading their extravagantly-dressed little ones like dogs at *Crufts*, parents and grandparents seem unaware of a spectacle going on above their heads. For them the sight of flocks of swallows screeching and swooping through those lofty tiered arches with breathtaking precision, is no big deal. It's just something that happens each evening since this great edifice was completed. Those pampered children in the square trussed up in their finery but longing for jeans and trainers, could only dream of such freedom.

Back at the campsite, we've parked next to a friendly retired English couple, who like me it transpires, are Laurie Lee 'fans' and each year spend six weeks touring Spain.

"Come and share a glass of *fino* later," our neighbour says, "the proprietor of a little vineyard at *Jerez* saves us a bottle of his special reserve every year".

"They probably say that to all the tourists!" but tact means that we keep this thought to ourselves.

Later, we sit discussing our travels and "*As I Walked Out One Midsummer Morning*", but I begin to have my doubts that they are *into* this book as much as I am.

"Of course, Laurie Lee spent the Civil War working behind a bar!" our neighbour declares.

"Well not according to *the book*!" I reply as though referring to the Bible.

They play their trump card.

"We went to a seminar about him."

I'm ashamed to say that the copious amounts of wine and that particularly potent *fino,* contribute to my irritation with these assertions.

"Have you actually *read* the book?" I ask, my voice rising to protect the reputation of my absent hero.

I know it is there in black and white: he **had** returned to fight for the cause. His subsequent work, *"A Moment of War"*, tells the story and joins George Orwell's *"Homage to Catalonia"* as witness to the tragedy of Civil War.

Harry for once leaps to my defence.

"Well if anyone knows what's in that book, it's my wife!" He assures them, dragging me back from the brink of another conflict.

I learn later that there had indeed been speculation about Mr. Lee's actual involvement in the war, but I prefer to stick to my own belief, thank you very much.

Wednesday 16th June

The day of our return to *La Granja* arrives, and I'm looking forward to returning there with mixed feelings, as this is to be the final place we intend to visit in Spain. The fountains we'd been looking forward to seeing are operated by water pressure from those mountains we drove across to get here, but a dry winter and spring has meant that reserves are in short supply. In consequence we will have to wait until the afternoon for this treat. Enough time then to make our farewells to the now familiar city of Segovia and its aqueduct and also visit nearby *San Ildefonsa*, home of the Royal Glassworks. We discover that the interest there has nothing to do with glass though, but the antics of argumentative storks nesting on redundant furnace chimneys above our heads.

At last the time comes for the palace to open. I make the mistake of saying I have a smattering of Spanish, when asked by the young woman who was to be our guide. This results in being baffled from one magnificent chandeliered room after another magnificent chandeliered room by a running commentary of extremely rapid and very incomprehensible Spanish.

"What's she saying?" I'm asked repeatedly by my Other Half. But of course I haven't a clue.

"Next time I'll keep quiet," I decide.

Rare and priceless collections of huge tapestries lining the walls are not quite up our street, but otherwise, it is a lovely place. Towards the end of the tour, an elegant elderly English-speaking Spanish lady decides to accompany us. She is keen to give us a history of her time spent in Britain but unfortunately none relating to that of the palace. But what an interesting life though, and to tell it would fill a whole library!

Up until she approaches us, a good-looking youth whom we assume to be a nephew or grandson seems to be her escort, but it turns out that the unlucky lad has been 'latched' onto also. His luck in losing his chaperone to us is our misfortune. There is still some time to spare before the long awaited fountains are to be turned on, and we intend to walk around as much of the grounds as possible beforehand. Being accompanied by this lady is becoming a liability. Despite being quite sprightly for her age, her pace is not suited to our intended swift tour. We don't wish to be impolite, but by wisely choosing a steep path up to the reservoir, this seems to do the trick. She's a lovely lady, but we have further to come than she, if we ever wanted to re-visit the Palace.

With the afore-mentioned low water levels, it's disappointing to find that only a few of the water features are operable. They will be operated individually and in turn, according to a notice board helpfully listing the order of display. There's much excitement as we arrive at the first fountain. During our perambulation of the gardens, quite a crowd has gathered with large school parties and coach-loads of pensioners creating a party atmosphere. Even a group of wimpled nuns have been caught up in this atmosphere.

With expectation and excitement buzzing all around us, we wonder what all the fuss is about. What could be so special about a few fountains? This first one looks ordinary enough: a large circular pool with various rococo sculptures placed strategically within it. Finding what we think is a good vantage point just behind some schoolchildren, we look on as two solemn-faced uniformed custodians approach a manhole, lift its wooden cover and begin to push and pull a large iron bar arrangement in it. Water begins to trickle lamely out of the ornaments.

I turn to Harry. "Hope it's going to be better than this!"

"They're a bit boring. No better than Trafalgar Square," he agrees, "and to think we've been hanging around for three days for this!"

But we speak too soon.

The youngsters begin to chant:

"*Más, más agua, más fuentes*"[1] and jump up and down madly waving their arms in the air.

It is then we realise what all the fuss is about. Suddenly water is everywhere. Those innocent-looking statues are spouting the stuff at least a hundred feet towards the sky, and anyone who has not taken the precaution of standing either under one of the surrounding trees or at a considerable distance away now looks like a drowned rat. The school kids obviously know exactly what is coming. They've positioned themselves for maximum saturation, but it's interesting to see how other onlookers physically challenged by age or inclination are transformed into svelte athletes to avoid a soaking. Even I'm surprised at how fast I make my getaway. Helpless laughter echoes around the grounds. We can't be the only people taken by surprise, but the children have got what they came for and are now doing an appreciative *'Mexican Wave'*. After a few minutes of this, the iron bar cranking ceases and the waters disappear almost as quickly as they had materialised.

The fun does not end there though. One of the men in uniform then produces a pole surmounted by a large red flag, and proceeds, pied-piper-like, to conduct the crowd to the next fountain. By now we are impressed with the whole experience, "It's the first time I've been in a carnival procession!" I exclaim.

Of course the subsequent *fuentes* cannot possibly have the same impact as that first one, but the young people remain determined to go home as wet as possible.

"I don't think their parents will be very pleased when they see the state of those expensive trainers," I remark to Harry.

A wonderful memento of that day is the photo we take of a group of these teenagers, arm in arm, soaked to the skin, but thoroughly happy. In the midst of the scrum, most noticeable is a pretty young girl wearing the headscarf denoting her Islamic faith, but obviously not inhibited by this. She is just as exhilarated and just as wet. Surrounded by Catholic friends she is simply one of the gang. Why can't different faiths always get on like that?

So ended our first tour of and our last day in Spain. If our initial impression of the country had been a disappointing one, we couldn't have wished for a better experience to end our visit with. We still had many miles to go before gaining the more familiar territory of France, but were certainly leaving feeling more upbeat about the place than we expected to only a few days before. Laurie Lee had marvelled at *La Granja* and its fountains, so had we, and it turned out to be one of the few places not to have become unrecognisable from the account of his travels.

Had our visit eased my obsession with Spain and Laurie Lee's book, *As I Walked Out One Midsummer Morning*? Many things had inevitably changed and some not for the better, as they had done in most places, but of course it depends on what you mean by better. All of Europe is now for the most part educated, well travelled and 'free'. There are many things in that country, particularly the attitude to the environment and bull fighting which are entirely unforgivable to my mind, but worse things, or at the very least things just as bad, happen everywhere. Nothing could have lived up to my expectations, but there-again if nothing about Spain had changed since Laurie's time there, then the world as a whole would be a terrible place.

Note (1) "More water, more fountains!"

Top Ten Tips

Ok. I'm not going to write chapter and verse on how to take a camper van abroad even though many have suggested I should. I'm not qualified, and experts would only butt in and tell me I've got it all wrong.

However, there are a few things I wish we'd known before plunging into life on the road that might be of use to those who are misguided and starry-eyed enough to take it up. So here goes.

One

Pack all your underwear in separate bags, e.g. his 'n hers.

Each bag should contain other bags containing different categories of undies. e.g. socks in one, pants in another (quite obvious really)

If you choose bags relevant to yourself and partner, this also helps instant identification.

For instance – I love shoes, clothes and books, so *NEXT* or *Waterstones* bags are great for my stuff, whereas my OH is more of a tools and compact disc person, so any *B & Q* or *HMV* wrapper is just perfect for his.

This bit of organisation enables a quick getaway in the morning if need be…it also avoids your precious under-garments being tipped out onto the floor by your travelling companion in his rush to get clean stuff to take over to the showers, before the Germans grab all the cubicles and hot water.

Two

Even though it may use up valuable space, take a fold-up table and chairs set.

This will enable you to take most of your meals outside (weather permitting) avoiding all the Baguette crumbs messing up the floor inside the van. You will also be helping to feed the local wild-life.

This tip was handed to us by some friends who took three young children to France in a hired van and spent much of their time sweeping up inside it.

Three

If your set-up doesn't have an awning, then get one. Apart from anything else, having a sheltered outside space makes your camper van feel so much bigger.

Many sites have no shade, and even if they do, it won't cover you for all of the day. The thought of sitting outside eating and soaking up the sun may be appealing during January in the UK, but the terrible heat of Spain is rather wearing if you get too much of it.

An awning is also handy for sheltering from the rain – though if it gets too windy, use a tying down kit (available from all good caravanning equipment places or study one they have for sale and make your own!) This in itself though may not be adequate if a real hoolie starts up, (please see chapter 'We've got a problem') so roll the whole thing up in that case. If you were a nautical type, you wouldn't put your boat sails up in a hurricane. An awning is very similar, so be warned.

The awning is the best part of your kit (apart from the on-board toilet if you have one) so look after it!

Also remember to wind it in before you leave a site...

Four

(This one is useful once you've embarked on your adventure)

Make a list of all the things on the van you need to check before leaving a site.

If you do make one, it also helps to look at it. Failing to do this will mean that before you've gone 100 yards, you will have to stop and anchor something down, turn off something or put up with a lot of clonking from things that should have been seen to while on terra firma.

As time wears on, you will have a list as long as you arm.

Five

Before you leave home, do some research.

In these days of the Internet it couldn't be simpler to find where campsites are. Get the REAL location of a site, rather than head for a town and drive round in circles trying to find it. Take it from me, this doesn't help relations with your travelling companion, so try to have as much info as you can.

The centre of Spain is particularly devoid of places to overnight officially, so either avoid it or know where you're heading. Even though you may stick to the coast, seeing a sign for a campsite might not necessarily mean it will be easy to find, so have the address and if the worst comes to the worst, ask a local (but as mentioned in my chapter, 'On How to Find', not a group of ladies out for their evening *paseo*).

Oh and if you remember to take a compass, make sure it points to the North...

Six

Take a screwdriver.

Seven

In fact, take a tool kit, string, super-glue and Duck tape.

Handy too are those thick stretchy rope things with a hook on both ends, though I'm not sure of the technical term for them. (Bungies?)

These have multiple uses and I can't recommend them too highly.

Eight

This tip will help ensure you are not left without things to eat or drink when the least excuse causes everywhere to batten down the hatches.

Try to obtain a list of Saint's days or other *Jours Feriés* especially if you intend to travel through France, Switzerland or any other predominantly Catholic country.

Local elections will have the same impact, that is, everywhere will be shut. Religious places like the Vatican museums are even worse, and doors are firmly closed to Jo Public for every kind of holy day you can think of plus many you can't.

In France there is usually a local *Boulangerie* open no matter what, the French cannot be without their *baguettes* for a day, but elsewhere cannot be guaranteed.

Nine

Obviously take a language dictionary or two, but don't rely on them too much.

Letting a local point to the word they mean can cause confusion.

(See chapter *"No Woman, No Cry"*)

Ten

Friday afternoons and evenings are popular times for the local population of nearby towns and cities to flock to campsites within a reasonable driving distance for a long weekend break. You will have to arrive before midday if you want to guarantee a pitch.

If you are within several hours drive from the Benelux countries, the same applies. The worst sites for this are those on the Swiss/Italian border, where you may have to compete with dozens of mainly Dutch caravans for a place. They are fierce competitors so be warned!

And Finally...

If you decide that this is not the life for you and sell your campervan, I suggest you spend the money on a cruise to New York on the Queen Mary 2. No more map-reading, no more dodgy campsites. You'll never again hanker after life on the road ... but it was fun while it lasted, wasn't it?

Lightning Source UK Ltd.
Milton Keynes UK
11 April 2011

170708UK00002B/160/P